MW00936216

Dolphin Girl

(Dolphin Trainer Mysteries #1)

by

Tracey V. Williams

First Electronic Edition: December 2017

First Print Edition: December 2017

eBook & Print book design & formatting by D. D. Scott's LetLoveGlow Author Services

Cover Illustration by Tracey V. Williams

Dedicated to all the dolphins who graced my life while I had the brief, though extraordinary, opportunity to work with them years ago. Some are still with us and some have swum to the other side. They will all live in my heart and dreams forever.

Thank you to my own pod whose love and support helped bring this story to fruition.

Chloe Martin loves dolphins and her dog Gabe. She's a Senior Trainer at Dolphin Connection, a Southern Florida marine mammal facility. But when she discovers the dead body of the facility's lead researcher in the women's restroom, her past as an amateur sleuth all at once becomes very much a part of her present, as well as the handsome detective assigned to the case.

In this YA Mystery, the first in a series, there's a murder to solve, lots of dolphins and a sweet dog to love and a romance that fairytales are made of. With a beautiful Christian element, it also delivers life lessons on faith and unconditional love and explores the deep bond sisters share.

Table of Contents

Dolphins - A poem....1
Chapter 1....3
Chapter 2....7
Chapter 3....11
Chapter 4....13
Chapter 5....17
Chapter 6....22
Chapter 7....26
Chapter 8....33
Chapter 9....40
Chapter 10....49
Chapter 11....64
Chapter 12....70
Chapter 13....78
Chapter 14....81
Chapter 15....91
Chapter 16....96
Chapter 17....104
Chapter 18....110
Chapter 19....123
Chapter 20....141
Chapter 21....148
Chapter 22....155
Chapter 23....174
Epilogue....187
Dolphin Fun Facts....193
About the Author....200
Books by Tracey V. Williams....201

Dolphins

Dolphins, dolphins of the sea,
You are so beautiful to me!

Your flips in the sky make us all stop and stare,
You swim underwater without any air!

You travel in a group called a pod,
Moms and aunts raise the calves which isn't odd!

Your signature whistles are like an individual name,
You recognize each other by them because no two are the same.

You are streamlined to swim with great speed and amazing grace,
Against other sea creatures you often win the race!

Your 88 cone-shaped teeth are neat,
Yet you swallow your fish whole and don't miss a beat!

You receive all your water in your fish,
At least you don't have to drink from a dish!

Your tails are unique and super strong,
They move up and down fast when the distance is long!

You love to dive down deep, rough house and play,
We could watch you spin and speed all day!

You breathe through a blow hole that opens up top,
Then it closes when you go underwater without a stop.

Your dorsal fin gives you all great balance,
And your pectoral fins are for steering with allowance.

You have a belly button on your tummy,
This is because you grew into a baby inside your Mummy.

When you are born your Mom nurses you with milk,
You have several whiskers on your rostrum which look like silk!

We will try our best to keep your water clean,
We are deeply sorry for the people who have been mean.

You deserve the cleanest water without any fishing line or trash,
When that stuff gets in your way it can create a very bad gash.

We'll work hard to clean up your waters and do our best,
Please know that we always want to pass your test!

By Tracey V. Williams

Chapter 1

The late afternoon sun was still bright as Chloe Hope Martin sat on the dock and watched the dolphins play together. Cali (the mother) and Emma (the aunt) were busy with the newest additions to their family at the marine mammal facility — two baby, Atlantic Bottlenose Dolphins named Alexa and Sophie. Cali and Emma were keeping an eye on them, bringing them a bit closer to the dock each day. Chloe would simply have to wait until the older females were ready to introduce her to the adorable babies she now watched from a distance.

Dolphins rarely have twins, and so Cali's pregnancy had been a fragile one. Chloe, along with the other trainers and veterinarians, kept watch on Cali throughout, but she handled it beautifully.

Even during the birth, she seemed to understand that time was of the essence, delivering the first calf and safely pushing it to the surface for a breath and then quickly delivering the second calf. Fortunately, dolphins are born tail first, so their blow hole where they take in oxygen is not exposed to the water until the final stage of delivery.

Patience was nothing new to Chloe. With many personal sacrifices along the way, she had worked a long time to become a trainer and knew she'd have to wait awhile still before she could begin to interact with Alexa and Sophie. That was fine. She enjoyed sitting on the dock just before evening, basking in the Florida sun. It was her favorite time of day. Almost everyone else had gone home, and the dolphins were having “dolphin time.”

Now, she was simply an observer — soaking in the sun and enjoying the view.

She leaned back on the dock and closed her eyes for a few moments. It wasn’t too late in the day to work on her tan, and she felt right at home so close to the water and the dolphins.

Actually, she was a long way from home. Or at least what used to be home. As a native New Yorker, she had always called the Big Apple her city. But for now, she was happy in her new surroundings. The west coast of Florida suited her well. There was culture, great restaurants, good shopping and most importantly — the dolphins.

It hadn’t been an easy trip getting here, though. She had relied on faith to guide her through the amazing adventure. That said, she had followed the same path as so many other dolphin trainers. She attended Dolphin Camp classes throughout her teenage years, studied marine biology and psychology in college and interned at a marine mammal facility the summer she graduated. As a result of her outstanding dedication during her internship, she got herself hired as an assistant trainer at Dolphin Connection, where she still worked.

Until recently, she had always held a second job, too — waitressing — as a trainer’s salary wasn’t always enough to pay the bills. She didn’t mind the extra hours as long as they kept her above water financially and in the water with the dolphins.

Ever since she was a little girl, Chloe had loved dolphins. She’d dreamed of working with them someday and asked for her dream to come true each night in her prayers. Sometimes, she couldn’t believe it actually happened.

She opened her eyes quickly now, just to make sure she wasn't dreaming, noticing with delight that the dolphins and palm trees were really there.

At an early age, her aunt had set her dream in place when she took Chloe on a special trip to Sea World. Chloe watched the Shamu Show through a ten-year-old's eyes and vowed to herself that someday she would become a trainer.

As a huge splash of water covered her on the dock, she snapped out of her daydreams. She sat up and looked around for the culprits. Emma, Cali, Alexa and Sophie were all at the dock making lots of noise out of their blowholes. Chloe looked down at them, surprised to see how close to the dock they were staying with the calves. They continued splashing and talking loudly, trying to get her attention.

Everything seemed to be fine with these girls themselves, so Chloe quickly scanned the rest of the lagoon to check on the other dolphins. She ran to each of the other seven separate lagoons and made sure that all 22 of the dolphins were okay. There didn't appear to be any problems at their fences or in the water. Since Dolphin Connection was a facility on the coast, sometimes nurse sharks slipped into the lagoons or kayakers got too close to the fences surrounding the facility and spooked the dolphins.

When Chloe was convinced everything was okay, she returned to the front lagoon and waved goodbye to the girls. She shrugged at them and said, "I'm sorry, girls, but I can't figure out what's bothering you ladies." Maybe they just wanted me to be on my way home, she said to herself, as she headed to the trainer's office to grab her bags.

She had gladly accepted the job of being "the late person" in charge of closing down because she liked the quiet time with the dolphins. She checked each of the office buildings to make sure they were locked, checked the dolphin lagoons again and headed for the employee gate.

The new restrooms that had been installed close to the front lagoons for the convenience of the facility guests caught her attention, and she decided to stop off. She needed to go grocery shopping before going home, and she knew she would never make it all that time without using the restroom first. She ducked into the door marked with a pink dolphin for women and flicked on the light. As she opened the door to the first stall, she was horrified to see a body slumped over the toilet.

Chapter 2

Chloe immediately recognized the body in front of her. It was Molly Green, the new head researcher who had only been at the facility about six months. When she saw the body, Chloe screamed and quickly ran to call for help.

As she ran, she considered whether or not she should have checked Molly's neck for a pulse, but decided it was better to get the paramedics there as soon as possible. Chloe was not good in medical emergencies, and she wasn't sure if she could have managed to get close enough to Molly's body to check for a pulse anyhow. There was a lot of blood. Molly appeared to have been shot at close range.

Chloe reached the trainer's office and fumbled for her keys in her backpack. As she pulled them out and put the key in the lock, her hand shook, and she had trouble opening the door. It occurred to her then that whoever killed Molly might still be on the grounds and that she was in imminent danger herself. Maybe that's why the dolphins had been agitated.

Chloe finally got the door open and locked herself in the office before she ran for the phone. She punched in 9-1-1 on the dial pad and quickly heard the emergency operator on the other end. Chloe gave her full name and present location and told the operator how she had found Molly's body in the bathroom. The operator told her that help was on the way and that she would talk to her until the police and emergency vehicles arrived. The operator kept her busy by asking her questions about the dolphins, her favorite subject, which she gladly answered.

After what seemed like an eternity, but was only about five minutes, Chloe heard sirens nearby. She quickly hung up on the operator as it dawned on her that the Police and EMS didn't have access to the grounds. The normal guest entrance through the gift shop was closed now, and the employee gate was locked.

Chloe ran for the employee gate which led to the parking lot and yelled to two policemen who were searching for a way in. They acknowledged her presence and called the others over as she reached the gate, opened it and hurriedly led them all to the bathroom. EMS rushed inside as the policemen began to secure the site, quickly starting to surround the restroom building with yellow crime scene tape.

It wasn't long before the EMS emerged from the Ladies' Room and radioed in that the victim was DOA. Chloe let out a shriek and heard screams behind her as well. She turned to see that Emma, Cali, Alexa and Sophie were at the edge of the lagoon closest to the restroom building and had let out their own dolphin noises when they heard her scream. She quickly ran over to calm them and reassure them that everything would be okay.

One of the detectives who had arrived on the scene came over to check on her. By that time, she had made her way down to the dock to be closer to the girls. The detective, which Chloe recognized by his plain clothes, was a good looking, young man who immediately caught her attention. She felt a pang of quiet guilt for noticing how handsome he was while her co-worker lay dead forty-feet away.

He hesitated at the edge of the dock, and Chloe motioned for him to step down. She told him to be careful, that the dock could be shaky. When the dock wobbled as his first foot touched down, he looked terrified.

Sensing his discomfort, Chloe smiled and reached out her hand to steady him. When he accepted her hand, she was shocked. She motioned for him to sit on the edge of the stationary, wooden platform that led down to the dock, and he seemed rather grateful for her suggestion.

She sat down next to him, and he introduced himself. His name was Brian White, and he was the Crime Scene Investigator at the local Sheriff's Office. He needed Chloe to recount as much as she could about what had happened that evening.

She told Officer White about her usual routine. She explained that she had lingered longer than usual, resting on the docks that evening, then searched the lagoons when the girls had become agitated before she began her usual closedown procedure. She told him that she had only decided to stop at the bathroom after she remembered she had to drop by the grocery store for dog food and dinner and realized she'd never make it if she didn't stop first. It was then that she found Molly's body and ran back to the trainer's office to call for help.

Officer White wrote down everything she said and looked up when Chloe stopped talking. He turned and asked her if that was it and gave her a brief smile. His dimples lit up his face for just a moment, and Chloe felt goose bumps run up and down her body. As she responded to his question, she shivered and was embarrassed when he asked her if she was cold. She tried to shrug off his concern, telling him she was just overwhelmed by all that had happened.

But it was so much more than that. Chloe couldn't shake the feeling that Molly's death had not been a random act of violence. Her gut instincts had proven correct in the past, and she was afraid she was right again. The air around her was filled with an ominous energy that led her to believe something personal and vile had occurred on the grounds of her beloved second home.

As it dawned on her that Shannon and Theresa, the owners of Dolphin Connection, needed to be contacted and informed about this unfortunate event, she jumped up. As she jumped to her feet, the dock shook and Officer White looked scared to death, once again. She steadied herself and the dock and reached out her hand to help Officer White to solid ground, telling him she needed to call her bosses right away.

Chapter 3

Chloe found herself in the trainer's office frantically looking for Shannon and Theresa's numbers. It dawned on her that she should have called them immediately after dialing 9-1-1.

She reached Theresa easily, who followed the same routine each day. She arrived at Dolphin Connection at 7AM and left at 5PM, seven-days-a-week. She went home for dinner and to continue her work in her private study. And that's exactly where she was when Chloe phoned her. She informed her she would be over to the facility in five minutes and asked her to please try and track down Shannon.

Chloe dialed Shannon's home phone number and talked to her oldest daughter Sue, who told her that her Mom had briefly stopped by home for a shower and change of clothes right after work, then she had taken off for the store. Sue said her Mom hadn't been specific about where she was going shopping or when she would be getting home. Chloe thanked the teenager for her help, left a short message and tried Shannon on her cell phone. Her voicemail popped up after just one ring, so Chloe left her a message, letting her know she was needed at the facility as soon as possible.

Chloe put down the phone, locked up the trainer's office and returned to the crime scene to wait for Theresa to arrive. The Police were busy looking for clues in the surrounding area of the restroom and dusting the women's room itself for fingerprints. Once she had been pronounced officially dead by the coroner, EMS had removed Molly's body. Chloe was told that the body would be taken to the hospital morgue until her family members were contacted and could positively identify her.

A few moments later, Theresa arrived on the scene, said hello to Chloe and started to talk to Officer White and his partner. She seemed her usual self — calm, professional and aggressive. She started firing questions at Officer White and his partner, a man Chloe overheard to be named Officer Doherty. Both officers motioned for Theresa to slow down and asked her to sit as well.

Chloe sat down with the other officers, well-within earshot. It seemed as if they had all forgotten she was there, and she certainly didn't want to interrupt them. Officer White asked Theresa if she and her sister Shannon were equal partners at the facility, and Theresa replied they were Co-Directors of Dolphin Connection and their father was the CEO. The officers said they would need to speak to Shannon and Mr. Ronald McLeod, their father, ASAP.

Theresa asked the officers to tell her everything they had learned so far and that she would continue to try and track down her sister, who was certainly in the area, she assured them, and her father who was out in California.

Eventually, Officer White glanced in Chloe's direction and motioned for her to come over. He said that she was free to go home as long as Theresa didn't need her for anything else. Theresa abruptly stood up, hugged Chloe and thanked her for how calmly she had handled the situation. She told her to go home and get some rest and that they would talk in the morning.

Chapter 4

Chloe walked out of the facility through the employee gate and quickly made her way to her car. As it was early January and after 8PM, it was pitch dark. The parking lot was eerily quiet.

She opened up the door to her Mustang, threw in her bag and shut the door, mindlessly making her way to the local grocery store. She loved the grocery stores in Florida. They were so big and so clean compared to the tiny, rather dingy NYC markets. She parked her car, grabbed a cart and went straight for the dog food aisle, trying to focus on the task at hand instead of what she'd just been through. Her apricot miniature poodle, Gabriel (Gabe for short), was out of all of his goodies. She grabbed his organic food, dry and wet, his rawhide chewies and cookies.

Gabe would already be upset because she was late, and he'd be anxiously waiting for his dinner. She didn't need too many other things, maybe some hot dogs, corn on the cob and chocolate milk. She moved quickly through the store. All she wanted to do at this point was get home. What was a satisfying day at first had turned into a nightmare.

It was a short drive home from the store, and Chloe knew the route so well she could have done it blindfolded. She pulled up to her house and carefully parked her car on the side of the driveway that was designated to be her space. She rented the upstairs from an older couple who had been married 35 years. She had a one-bedroom place, a small living room/kitchen area and a fabulous porch with a view of the Gulf of Mexico. The view had sold her on the place as soon as she saw it.

She had spent many hours on that porch reading, writing and relaxing. She couldn't imagine living anywhere else in the world. Her rent was affordable, dogs were allowed and her landlords loved her because she was quiet.

She climbed up the stairs to her apartment and could hear Gabe stirring at the door. He always knew when she arrived because he could hear her car coming down the street. He also expected her home at about the same time each day and was upset when she arrived late. It threw off his whole schedule. He loved to eat and had a fit if he didn't get his dinner on time. Since she loved to eat, too, and got a little grouchy herself if she missed a meal, Chloe couldn't blame him.

As she reached the top of her stairs and could see the front door clearly, the sensor on the porch light picked up her presence. She fumbled inside her pocketbook for her keys — she never had them ready to use, a habit that had good-humoredly annoyed her friends and family for years. Finally, she found them, opened the door and received the most wonderful greeting from Gabe. She wondered to herself, as she did each night when she got home, how anyone could live without a dog. There was nothing quite like the welcoming they gave you each time you walked in the door, even if you had left only five minutes before.

Chloe put on Gabe's leash, grabbed a baggie to use as a pooper scooper and took him on a long walk around the neighborhood. After being locked inside all day, he needed the fresh air and exercise, and after the events at work, she needed to clear her mind.

She still couldn't believe Molly was dead. She certainly couldn't fathom who would want her dead. She didn't think Molly had any enemies, none she knew of at least.

Well, she thought to herself, it's better to leave the questions to the detectives. Officer White seemed like a competent professional who would solve the case and bring justice for Molly.

Just the thought of Officer White brought about a flurry of butterflies in her stomach. She quickly changed her thoughts to a new subject.

After a nice, half-hour walk, Gabe and Chloe returned home. Chloe fed her grateful companion his dinner and decided to change into her pajamas before she had her own meal. Her stomach was still upset over what she had seen in the bathroom. Molly's lifeless body slumped over the toilet wasn't a sight she would soon forget.

She shook her head and tried to shake herself of the scene. She pulled out her favorite jammies, and slipped them on, picked up the phone and slid under the covers of her bed.

She punched in the number for her best friend Grace, who still lived up in New York where they had grown-up together. Grace had married her high school sweetheart and now had two small children — Jackson, 3, and Kristen, 9-months. Grace was a full-time mom and proud of it. She spent a great deal of her time reading to and playing with her kids and taking care of all of their needs. Despite the hecticness of having two young children, she still kept a beautiful home, cooked every night and hosted business dinners for her husband. Grace had taught middle school until she had Jackson and was a well-respected teacher. She was happy to be at home now with her own children, especially since school environments had changed greatly since she first started teaching. She continued challenging her intellectual skills through writing, when she could find the time. She hoped to get her first children's book published within the next year.

Chloe listened as the line rang several times, but no one picked up on the other end. She hoped Grace would answer because she really needed to chat with her, but she knew she was probably in the middle of the kids' bedtime ritual. After eight rings, the answering machine picked up, and Chloe left a message. "Grace," she said, "call me back PLEASE! You'll never believe what happened to me today."

Chloe hung up the phone and hoped she hadn't sounded too urgent. She should have told Grace that everything was fine now, so not to worry, but she had already hung up and didn't want to leave another message. She knew better than to call one of her friends from work. That would just start a gossip chain. The trainers loved to gossip. Maybe it was because they worked with the animals all day who couldn't talk with them and they just needed to let it out. Regardless, Chloe thought it would be better if everyone at the facility found out about the murder the next day at work. And she sure hoped she could keep a low profile about her discovery of the scene.

Knowing that Gabe would be done with his dinner by now, Chloe went out to the kitchen to wash his bowl. She decided to make the hot dogs and corn for herself and sat down to watch a rerun of *Friends*. At least that would make her laugh. Just as the show was ending, the phone started ringing, and Chloe jumped up to answer it.

"Hello," she said in the most positive voice she could muster and was relieved to hear Grace's soothing New York accent on the other end.

Chapter 5

"Hi, is everything okay? You didn't find another dead body, did you?" Grace blurted out from the other end of the phone.

"I'm fine, I'm fine," Chloe said as she tried to calm Grace down as quickly as possible and assure her that it was not an emergency, even though she had come across yet another corpse.

"I'm sorry I didn't pick up earlier, but I was trying to get the kids to sleep, and I'm alone tonight. Matt had a late meeting, and it just isn't the same when he isn't home for bedtime," Grace explained.

"Don't worry. I knew I shouldn't have called you at such a bad time, but I just needed to vent," Chloe told her oldest and dearest friend.

At Grace's urging, Chloe began to recount her day, detail-by-detail. It was nice to have someone who was so willing and so eager to hear about her life. Every few minutes, Grace would add a "wow" or an "oh my God" to the conversation, but for the most part, she let Chloe speak without interruption. "After the detective and my boss said I was free to go, I went to the grocery store and came home. Then I called you."

Grace was silent for a moment, probably overwhelmed by all the information Chloe had given her.

"Grace, are you still there?" Chloe asked into the phone.

"I'm here," she piped up. "I was trying to take in everything you told me. It just doesn't make sense. Why would someone shoot a young researcher at a dolphin facility?"

"I have no idea," Chloe responded. "It makes no sense to me either. And something felt off, suspect I guess, at Dolphin Connection after I found the body. I can't put my finger on it, but the feeling won't stop nagging at me. Hopefully, I'll get some more information tomorrow at work."

"Did Molly have any close friends at the facility who might have some idea why someone might have wanted to hurt her?" Grace asked.

"Not really," Chloe responded. "She had only worked at the facility for about six months so far. She really didn't have time to get too close to anyone. She was quiet and professional and seemed to enjoy her work. She came to Dolphin Connection to expand on her Master's Thesis which she began several years ago under the guidance of the former Research Director."

"What was the project about?" Grace asked.

"They were researching the breeding practices of the facility and the genetic lines of each of the dolphins," Chloe explained. "Our facility, like many others, has been very active in breeding our own dolphins and successfully growing our dolphin family in a healthy manner for some time now. I know you've heard me talk about our dolphin calves over the years, including the adorable twins born this past year!"

"Yes, you talk about those twins *all* the time," Grace exclaimed.

"Can't help myself. There's nothing cuter than a dolphin calf or two!" Chloe said, her heart full of joy just talking about them.

"Except my babies," Grace retorted.

"Point taken!" Chloe said and laughed. "We'll call it a tie!"

"Just wait until your babies are born, you'll understand then."

"I'm sure you're right, my old, wise friend. But, we digress. There was a law passed on October 21, 1972 called the Marine Mammal Protection Act which made it illegal to collect dolphins or any other marine mammals from the wild. At the time, because of movies and television shows, the public had started to become very interested in dolphins and other marine animals and pushed for legislation to protect them from any intentional harm."

"I had no idea," Grace said.

"Most people have no idea about many of the laws that pertain to marine mammals," Chloe said, thinking how sad it was, but also more than true.

"Interesting," Grace responded. "By the way, what happened to the other researcher Molly had worked with?"

"Her name was Kelly Smith, and she had been at the facility around ten years when she resigned. When she was home for the holidays last fall, she reunited with an old flame and decided it would be easier to pursue the relationship if she returned to Massachusetts. She was in her early 30's, never married and desperately wanted a family. At the time, her move made total sense to me. She had been with the facility for a decade, and it was time for her to move on. It seemed to be a perfect transition between the two women because Kelly had trained Molly during her graduate work, and she was ready to take over the position by early July when Kelly took off. Molly has worked so hard since then to find her place at the facility, but I really hadn't gotten a chance to get to know her very well. I don't think anyone at the facility really knew her too well. She worked so hard that it didn't give her much time to socialize with the rest of us."

"I guess you'll find out more when her family comes down to identify the body," Grace replied.

"That's true," Chloe said. "That will surely be a hard trip for them to make."

"I can't even imagine," Grace said as her voice trailed off. "Hold on a moment…"

Chloe figured she probably heard one of the kids crying.

Grace came back to the phone, and before she could get it out, Chloe said, "I know. I know. You've got to run."

"Kristen is crying and has woken up Jackson, so I'm gonna have my hands full. Do you want me to call you back later?" She asked.

"Don't worry about it. I'm tired, and it's going to be a long day tomorrow. Thanks for listening, as always. You're the best."

"You know I'm always here," Grace said, "and I'll especially be thinking about you tomorrow. Your life certainly is more interesting than mine. While you are finding out about a murder victim, I'll be changing diapers and making miniature Minnie Mouse figurines out of Play-doh."

"I don't feel too sorry for you," Chloe offered and laughed. "You know I'd love to be in your shoes!"

"The grass is always greener on the other side," Grace said and sighed.

"You better run. I love you, and I miss you. Give the kids a big hug for me. And keep the faith."

"I will, as I know you will, too. And next time we talk, I want to hear a little more about this Detective White. He sounds interesting."

"Bye, Grace," Chloe snapped into the phone."

“Just thought I’d mention it,” Grace said and giggled. “And please don’t find another dead body. You seem to attract them. I know everything is part of God’s plan, but this part of his plan for you really concerns me. Be safe. Bye!”

“Bye,” Chloe said as she hung up the phone. She called Gabe and made her way into her bedroom, thoughts of Officer White flooding her head.

Chapter 6

Chloe woke early the next morning and decided to take Gabe for a jog since she had extra time. They both needed the exercise, she thought to herself, and it might help her to clear her head for the day ahead.

She had slept fitfully the night before, waking many times from dreams of seeing Molly's dead body slumped over the toilet. The last time it happened, she decided she might as well get up for the day.

She quickly pulled on a tank top and running shorts, grabbed Gabe's leash and the two of them headed out the door.

Her neighborhood was like a grid, so it was easy to know how far she went when she jogged. She and Gabe went straight down their street — Mango Court — and then turned right onto Hibiscus Drive. From there, they made another right on Orange Blossom and then a right onto Bougainvillea Street. That brought them back to Mango Court, and they were off on another loop. Five times around, they had completed their five miles and were both exhausted.

As they headed for the house, Chloe slowed down and allowed Gabe some well-deserved sniffing time. He could spend all day going from tree to bush to tree to see what other dogs had been around. For a small dog, he did his best to mark as high as he could. He actually did a handstand on his front paws to get his output higher than the other dogs. It made Chloe laugh, a deep belly laugh, every time he did it. Maybe that was part of the reason he continued to do it. He was so loyal. Everything he did seemed to be connected to her in some way or another. As she watched him, she laughed out loud and thought to herself that she didn't know what she would do without him.

She glanced at her watch and realized it was getting late. "Let's go, Gabe," she said as she nudged his leash to pry him away from his smells. He looked up at her to see just how intent she was to head home, and she beckoned him again. He realized his sniffing time was up and reluctantly started home.

As they were climbing up the stairs to the apartment, Chloe heard the phone ringing and pulled Gabe to rush upstairs with her. She made it inside and reached the phone just as the answering machine kicked on.

"Hi, hold on a second, and I'll turn off the machine," she said into the receiver. She fumbled to find the stop button as the Disney music she had at the beginning of her message blared into her ear and the ear of her caller.

"Sorry about that," she said as soon as she had gotten the message to stop.

"That's okay," came her boss's voice on the other end.

"This is Theresa, Chloe," her boss informed her as if she couldn't tell her distinctive, gruff voice anywhere. There was no mistaking her for someone else.

"Listen, Chloe, I spoke with Shannon this morning, and we both think it would be best if you keep quiet about what happened last night when you get to work today. Of course, everyone will be informed that Molly has died," Theresa continued, "but we just don't think anyone needs to know the details until the investigation is over. It looks so far as if this was just a freak accident. Probably a drifter or someone like that who got on the property somehow. Molly was in the wrong place at the wrong time."

"Really?" Chloe asked, interrupting her as politely as possible. "It seems odd that a drifter would have a silencer, even if a makeshift one, but one must have been used because I didn't hear a gunshot, and I was quite near the restroom when it happened. There was no audible sound from the direction of the crime scene that could be heard by a human ear. However, the dolphins sensed the disturbance. I guess we'll see what evidence turns up. Detective White seems very competent. I'm sure he'll figure out what happened."

"I'm sure he will, too," agreed Theresa, "and we'll do everything we can to help him with the investigation. In the meantime, for the sake of the dolphins, I don't want there to be a great deal of alarm at the facility today. If our employees don't feel comfortable, the care of our animals will be sacrificed. Detective White said this really looks like an isolated incident, and it would be best to keep our routine as normal as possible."

"I agree," Chloe piped in, always looking out for the dolphins' best interests. "If this was a freak accident, there is no reason to overly upset everyone. With three babies due soon, and Alexa and Sophie so young, of course our focus needs to be on the dolphins."

"I'm glad you understand," Theresa responded. "Thank you again for being so calm and collected last night, Chloe. I can't think of anyone who could've handled such an unfortunate situation like you did. We are so lucky to have you. You treat the dolphins as if they are your own children."

"Theresa, Gabe and all of the dolphins are my children. Even when I have a human family of my own, they'll still be my children. You know how much I love them.

Speaking of which, I need to get showered and into work. I'm on the first session this morning, and I don't want to be late. Cali and Emma are starving in the morning from taking care of the twins."

"I'm sorry to have held you up. I'll see you when you get in. Thanks again, Chloe."

"No problem," Chloe told her boss as she said goodbye and hung up the phone.

That was nice of her to call, Chloe thought to herself. She should be sainted for all she has done for those animals, and she hoped that maybe someday somebody would say the same thing about her.

She totally understood why Theresa would want to keep things as normal as possible for the sake of the dolphins. Nonetheless, something tugged at her gut, and she wondered if there was more to the situation than met the eye.

This wasn't the first dead body to cross her path, and if her past was any indicator, she wouldn't be able to keep her nose out of this case, either. A crime was like an interesting puzzle to her — one she couldn't help but try to piece together and solve. And if this was a crime, it was personal. It involved one of the Dolphin Connection family members, and it had taken place on the grounds of their beloved facility. Chloe would be more motivated than ever to find answers and restore order to her world.

Chapter 7

Chloe jumped in her Mustang and started out for the facility as she did each morning. She stopped at the bagel store and got her usual, a sour dough toasted with butter. They knew her well at the shop. She had stopped there each morning for the last ten years she had worked at Dolphin Connection. Sometimes, she even stopped again in the afternoon. Living in New York during her childhood, Chloe grew up on bagels and she really couldn't start a day without one.

She pulled into the parking lot and carefully found a spot. She was still cautious around Floridian drivers. She'd never get used to them even after learning how to drive in NYC when she was interning at Midtown Galleries. She found her spot, usually the same one each day, and made the short walk up the ramp to the Bagels on Broadway Store.

"Hey, Greg!" Chloe yelled over to the owner of the shop as she grabbed her orange juice out of the refrigerator.

"How's my favorite girl?" Greg called out.

Chloe smiled and walked over to the counter.

Greg greeted her with his usual hug and asked her about her day ahead. Greg and his wife Ann were also native New Yorkers. They had made the move down to Florida about twelve years earlier, and Greg had brought his recipe for NY bagels with him. His two grown sons still lived in New York, and so Greg had sort of taken Chloe on as a surrogate daughter. He knew how much she missed her parents, and it fulfilled his desire to have a daughter of his own.

Greg listened as Chloe described her day ahead. "First, I have sessions this morning with Cali and Emma. I'll have them do some light training work, maybe some front and back dives and tail walks. Now that Alexa and Sophie are getting a little older, I've gotten them interested in doing some behaviors again. For a while there, they were just swimming by the dock for their fish."

"Not a bad deal," added Greg.

"Not at all," Chloe agreed, "but it is time for them to get in shape again. It is most important that Cali take good care of Alexa and Sophie and nurse them regularly, but it is also important that she stay in shape for her own health. After my session with my favorite girls, I have a short break and then a medical demo with Tango & Cash and Sugar & Spice for the next tour group of the morning. In the afternoon, I am the lucky one who gets to introduce our new Dolphin Learner students to our dolphin family and the layout of our grounds so that they feel at home during their stay. We'll visit everywhere from the fish house to the offices to the gift shop."

Chloe didn't need to remind Greg after all these years that Dolphin Learners was a week-long educational program for students of all ages from many areas of the world, one of the special programs that set Dolphin Connection apart from other facilities.

"What kind of Dolphin Learners group do you have this week, Chloe?" Greg asked.

"We've got an adult group with participants from all over the country. Young and old alike, everyone comes with a passion for dolphins, and they are always a joy to teach. Whether they are just starting their careers or finally have a chance to pursue their dreams, they eagerly want to learn everything they can. I'm going to have lunch with the students and talk to them about how I got involved in training as well," Chloe responded.

"Didn't have to make your own lunch today, huh?" Greg laughed. He knew Chloe didn't stock her fridge, at all.

"No, and you know it's a great deal for me when I get to eat with the students. A home cooked meal at the dorm and nice company? Sweet! I'll be well-fed before my late afternoon sessions. I'm doing the 3 PM show with the boys, Siesta and Sunset. That is always a ball to do, and the crowd loves the way they perform to the beat of the music. Then, I'll have a couple of final play sessions to finish off the feeding needs for the day. Eventually, I'll relax and work on my records before I close up for the day."

"Not a bad day, huh?" Greg pointed out as he handed her a bagel.

"You say that everyday, Greg," Chloe replied as she took the bagel and gave Greg the $2.25 she paid each morning for her breakfast.

A couple of customers entered the shop as she finished paying, and so she hugged Greg and thanked him for caring so much about her life, as she did each morning, and waved goodbye as she headed for the door. She knew how lucky she was to have he and Ann look after her. It not only made her feel special, but safe, too. She knew if she didn't show up for her bagel in the morning, Greg would certainly alert the local police. For that reason, if she was sick and couldn't get to the store, which was a very rare occasion, she called to let him know so that he wouldn't worry. Ann and Greg were like her guardian angels here on Earth, special individuals whom God had placed in her life with a purposeful intention.

As she walked out to her car, Chloe shook her OJ and opened the container. She got herself seat-belted in and opened-up her bagel on her lap. She had never been able to wait until she got to work to eat her breakfast. As she drove the twenty minutes it took to get to work, she wolfed down the bagel.

It was an easy drive, and Chloe enjoyed the time to listen to music and collect her thoughts for the day. Many of her friends thought she was crazy to drive that far, but it was nothing to Chloe. It was well worth it. As if the salty scents that drifted through her open windows while she slept weren't enough, the spectacular turquoise hues that graced her eyes each time she made this trip were magnificent. The views she was afforded from her apartment and workplace being located so close to the water were spectacular. Occasional sightings of wild dolphins and manatees were icing on the cake. She loved seeing marine mammals thriving in their natural habitat as did most people who worked with them.

Chloe made it to the facility with no problems and pulled into the employee parking lot. She was due in at 8:30AM and it was only 8:10AM, so she had plenty of time to get over to the office. She couldn't remember a day when she had ever been late. It was like her second home, and she was always eager to get there.

When she crossed through the employee gate and headed for the front lagoon, she wasn't sure what to expect. She was curious to see if the crime scene tape was still around the restroom facility. When she rounded the corner and discovered that not only was the tape gone, but anyone who was not on the premises the night before would have no reason to suspect that anything had happened there, she was shocked.

The early crew was already in the water taking care of some of the special needs dolphins who didn't eat very well. Chloe waved to them as she walked in the direction of the trainer's office.

Thanks to Theresa, the trainer's office had been totally refurbished a few years earlier. Mr. McLeod and Shannon hadn't thought the expensive renovations were necessary, but Theresa insisted on the updates. She always looked out for her staff and the dolphins.

The new trainer's office had individual workstations with desks and computers for each of the twelve trainers. There was also a state-of-the-art media center for the trainers to watch new educational videos or listen to their favorite music. There was a small kitchenette as well so that the trainers could bring their own lunch each day. There was even a comfortable couch where many of them rested their tired bodies after a long day in the hot Florida sun.

Chloe had been very involved in the renovations. She helped Theresa pick out the furniture and design the layout of the room. Chloe had been an art history minor in college, and she loved to decorate whenever she could. She also spent a great deal of her time painting dolphins, her favorite subject, and had brought several paintings into the office to hang on the bare walls.

She pulled open the door to the trainer's office and smiled at the thought of how well she and Theresa had done with the room. There wasn't anyone inside, so she threw down her bags on her desk and checked to make sure her schedule hadn't changed.

Their schedule was displayed on a large computer screen at the front of the office. Theresa worked on it from home each afternoon and then faxed it over to the office. Since Chloe always closed-up in the evening, she took the responsibility of scanning the fax once Theresa sent it in and made sure it was displayed for the other trainers when they arrived each morning. That way, too, Chloe always had the advantage of knowing her schedule for the next day before she went home at night. The other trainers didn't know the details of their day until they arrived at the facility.

Even on her days off, Theresa paid Chloe the courtesy of sending a copy of the schedule to her private email. Her dedication did not go unrewarded.

Chloe noticed that the schedule had changed slightly, so she was glad she'd checked it. It seemed the Dolphin Learners were supposed to have a Research Seminar before she took them for a Meet-and-Greet with their dolphin family and a tour of the grounds. She had been substituted for Molly to teach it. She was surprised because she really didn't know much about the Research Seminar.

"Hi," said Theresa as she came through the door.

Chloe turned to greet her boss.

"Are you okay with that change? I can get Molly's material for the Research Seminar, and I'll make sure you have enough time to review it before this afternoon. I didn't want to cancel the class because the students had really been looking forward to it," Theresa commented.

"That's fine," said Chloe. "I'm sure I can handle it."

"You can handle anything, Chloe, you should know that by now."

"Thanks," Chloe said as she headed back to her desk to look at the letter that Theresa had put there and on the desks of the other trainers.

"That is the official letter about Molly's death," Theresa offered as she saw Chloe begin to read it. "We thought it would be the best way to handle the matter. This way, everyone has the correct information first thing in the morning, and there doesn't have to be any gossip. I mentioned at the end that I would like the staff to come up with some sort of a memorial to honor Molly. Let me know if you have any ideas."

"I will," replied Chloe and waved goodbye as Theresa left the office. She quickly got herself together and ran out the door. She had just a few moments left before her first session.

Chapter 8

As Chloe rushed down to the dock, she was greeted by her favorite bunch of girls. She was happy to see that they were doing fine even after the chaos of the previous night.

When she got to the fish house, the coolers were ready for her as a group of very energetic volunteers had arrived early that morning. She picked up one for each of the dolphins, each labeled with one of their names and with the correct type and amount of fish in them for their respective diets.

After she set down the coolers, Chloe knelt on the dock and put her hands in the water to greet Emma, Cali, Alexa and Sophie. She gave Emma and Cali a few back rubs, as Alexa and Sophie stayed just out of reach. She then stood up and gave them the signal for a front dive, and they took off with Alexa and Sophie in their wake. Chloe blew her whistle just as the dolphins successfully completed their dives. Alexa and Sophie attempted mini-dives next to them. They quickly swam back to the dock for their fish reward. There was nothing like a couple of big, fat herrings to wake up the girls in the morning!

Now that the calves were a little older, Cali was back to a pretty normal training schedule. When the calves were very young, it was important for her to nurse them and watch over them. Now, she was able to care for them and train at the same time. Cali, like all Atlantic Bottlenose

Dolphins, needed the physical and intellectual stimulation of training.

Before Chloe knew it, a tour guide was leading a group of guests to the facility down the boardwalk as they anxiously awaited to see the newest and youngest members of Dolphin Connection. There was no doubt about it, everybody loved a baby dolphin. At around 4-feet long and 75 pounds, there was nothing more adorable than that small, shining, grey face. Alexa and Sophie won the hearts of all the people who came to see them. It didn't matter that they didn't do much yet in the way of trained behaviors. Guests simply enjoyed seeing them swim around in their mother's slip, nursing, and occasionally popping up near the dock.

Emma and Cali eyed the tour group approaching and anxiously looked to Chloe for their next signal. She sent them out for a flying forward tail walk in the direction of the oncoming crowd, who clapped and cheered as the girls hoisted their bodies out of the water. Chloe blew her whistle and Emma and Cali returned to the dock for their rewards, one big, fat herring each. Alexa and Sophie came over as well, and Chloe gave them each a small herring from their own cooler just for being there.

Chloe and the girls gave a great show for the tour group, and the girls ate all of their fish, as usual. Chloe gave each of them their last fish at the same time, and when their coolers were empty, she dumped the remaining ice to show the curious dolphins that their meals were done. She said goodbye to Emma, Cali, Alexa and Sophie and promised she would see them later.

For now, she was in a rush to get back to the office and see if there was any talk of Molly's death despite the fact that the staff had been asked to keep quiet. Chloe knew someone wouldn't be able to resist the urge to talk, and she was very curious to find out why Molly had met such an unfortunate fate. Chloe didn't want to believe it was intentional, and she wouldn't rest until she found out the truth, either way.

If all else failed, she would have to do a little investigating of her own. Maybe some detective work would bring her in touch with Detective White, she thought, and then felt guilty once again for having that thought after witnessing such a gruesome scene the night before.

She quickly walked to the fish house to thoroughly wash the coolers she had just used and let them dry so that they could be filled for the girls' afternoon meals. It was busy in the fish house as the volunteers were cleaning and checking piles of fish that would be used throughout the day.

She remembered the time when she was an intern and how she had spent many, many hours in the fish house. She felt as if she were always covered in fish scales. It had taught her so much, though, about the operation of the facility, and she remembered the times with appreciation. She knew what went into the daily fish and vitamin preparation for the dolphins and the energy it took to keep the fish house totally sanitized, and she never took it for granted. Once her buckets were cleaned, she thanked the volunteers who were in the fish house at the time for their hard work and dedication and headed out the door to her office. There was no time to waste. She had a Research Class to go over and learn about for that afternoon!

Chloe got back to the office and was relieved to be in the air conditioning and at her desk for a few moments. As promised, Theresa had delivered the notes for the class. Chloe picked up the folder and started to browse through it. She had attended the seminar years ago when she first started working at Dolphin Connection, but it was clear that it had been greatly expanded. She wondered to herself if Molly had been the one to put the work into changing the outline. Whoever was responsible had clearly spent a great deal of time researching new information and resources.

If it had been Molly, that wouldn't have surprised Chloe. Molly was always working. From the day she arrived at DC, she could usually be found on the computer, in the library or reading through the information files on each of the dolphins and the history of the facility. She seemed to be very interested in how DC had gotten off the ground. She seemed especially interested in the heritage of where each dolphin was born. Were they collected from the wild before the Marine Mammal Act of 1972 when it was still legal to do so, or were they born in human care with the details of their lineage recorded?

Since Molly had been working on some sort of project, there had to be files stored in her office. Chloe made a mental note to look for them. Molly had interviewed many of the long-term employees at Dolphin Connection who were treasure troves of information about the facility in general, but she hadn't interviewed Chloe yet.

It seemed likely that Molly was doing research of a sensitive nature because Shannon, who was in charge of research, conferenced with her a lot and seemed a little nervous around her lately. While both sisters claimed to have their hearts in the right place in regard to keeping the facility running smoothly and the dolphins functioning in good health during this sensitive time, Chloe couldn't let go of her nagging feeling that they seemed a little too much in a rush to keep Molly's death quiet.

Chloe couldn't worry about that now; she had a busy afternoon. First, she would review the research material in the few minutes she had before her next session, and then she would be off to eat lunch with the students. As the afternoon seminar leader, it was her job to spend some extra time with the students at meal time in order to answer their questions. Students usually wanted to ask questions about everything, but especially training. Most of them were trying to get into the marine mammal field and were hungry for as much information as they could get their hands on. Being that the field was so limited and there were so few job opportunities, the students really needed the hands-on treatment and background they received during their week-long camp at Dolphin Connection.

Chloe would advise the students that to be a trainer they should have an undergraduate degree in either marine biology or psychology. She would also let them know how important it was to volunteer or intern, or both, during school or when they graduated. She couldn't stress that point enough. It was almost impossible to get a position at a facility if you hadn't spent time there as a volunteer or an intern first. Chloe always let them know that even though the work was unpaid, it was well worth the experience.

Her time as an intern was one of the most memorable in her life. She met wonderful friends who she still kept in touch with on a regular basis.

She also learned more about the dolphins than she had in her four years at college. She gained invaluable knowledge of the way in which a marine mammal facility operated. She spent endless hours with the dolphins — learning their histories, their personalities and their diets.

She was ready to answer any question a guest or student had for her. Above all, she would let the students know that one had to be both a very strong swimmer and a team player to be a successful dolphin trainer.

When the door to the office slammed, she jumped, realizing she'd been daydreaming for quite some time. That often happened when she thought about the days she was an intern. They were such happy memories.

"What are you doing?" Rachel, a junior trainer, asked as she came around the corner and sat down at her desk.

"I'm just getting ready for the Research Seminar this afternoon," Chloe responded. "It was already scheduled, and Shannon and Theresa didn't want the students to miss out. Even though it isn't really my area of expertise, Theresa asked me to take it over. I thought they might just cancel it and explain about Molly's death last night, but they seem very intent on keeping a low profile about those events."

"So, how are you doing?" Rachel asked Chloe. "I mean, I heard some murmur that you were the one who found Molly's body. It must have been horrible!"

"How did you hear that?" Chloe asked, surprised that anyone would know that since she hadn't said a word to anyone other than Grace.

"Oh, just through the grape vine," Rachel replied, and gave a little smile.

Chloe didn't know what that was supposed to mean, but rather than let Rachel know of her perplexion, she smiled back and nodded in agreement.

Chloe couldn't imagine how Rachel had managed to get details about the murder so quickly, but like some of the other younger trainers, she made it her business to know everyone else's business. Chloe wondered what other information was circulating around the facility and how much people really knew. She got along with everyone at work, so it would be easy for her to get a handle on any rumors that were being passed around. And it sounded like she needed to.

"Chloe, are you ready to go?" Jenna, a fellow senior trainer, asked as she popped her head in the office. "We're on the next session together. It's a medical demo with Tango and Cash."

"I'll be right there. I'll meet you in the fish house in a moment. I just need to stop at the restroom. The boys will be thrilled to do a med demo, huh?" Chloe said sarcastically.

"I know," replied Jenna. "It is their least favorite session. At least they'll be happy to see you — their name giver!"

Chloe laughed and nodded, "I like their names, no matter what anyone says! You know I've named all my dogs after characters in Sly Stallone's movies, so why not carry on the tradition with the dolphins? Rocky and Rambo were fitting names for my feisty poodles, and Tango & Cash certainly fit our daring duo out there in the far lagoon. And Gabe, the character he is named after in the Cliff Hanger movie, is a fiercely loyal guy. There is no creature more devoted than my Gabe! It's just plain fun and a bit sentimental for me to keep up the tradition, even if nobody else gets it or appreciates it."

"I know the whole story," Jenna said and laughed, "and they really are cute names. I just like teasing you because I get a reaction just like you gave me every time."

"Thanks a lot," Chloe responded and gave her a smile to show she, too, knew it was all in fun. "I'll see you in a moment in the fish house."

"I'll start to get the buckets ready to make it up to you," Jenna called as she headed out the door. "And on a serious note, I hope you are doing okay, Chloe. It is mindboggling that you stumbled upon another crime scene. And this time, right here on the grounds of Dolphin Connection."

Chapter 9

Chloe rounded the corner of the walkway and Tango & Cash immediately rejoiced over her arrival. They squealed and splashed and then sped around their lagoon. She showed the same enthusiasm for them in return which only hyped them up even more. What characters, she thought to herself, as she got down on their docks.

The boys popped right-up and she gave them their first hand signal for back dives. She stationed her left hand at her waist, palm facing the dolphins, thumb out, pointer up and the remaining 3 fingers curled down.

She then made that same hand into a fist and bent the fist to her left shoulder. Quickly, she straightened her arm out to the side and up at a 45-degree angle while keeping her hand in a fist.

The boys took off together and both came up for their first back dive at the same time. At the completion of their dive, Chloe blew her whistle and they returned to the dock. The whistle was their signal that they had done their dive correctly and should come back to the dock for a reward. In training terms, this is called a bridge.

Chloe threw Tango & Cash each a large herring and sent them out for spiral dives. She loved the way the boys twisted and turned when they did their spirals, and she belly-laughed as she watched their bodies launch and twist through the air. She let them do four dives this time until she bridged them. Upon her whistle, they zoomed back to the dock.

As she trained Tango & Cash, Jenna was busy in the same lagoon with Sugar & Spice. She was having just as much fun as Chloe. The trainers all believed that they truly had the best jobs in the world.

Tango & Cash and Sugar & Spice shared a lagoon because they were "dating" one another. The facility believed strongly in having a large family of dolphins, though never more than fit comfortably at Dolphin Connection. Since it was illegal to collect marine mammals from the wild, the facility focused on breeding their own dolphins and taking in dolphins from other sites, like aquariums, who needed the type of special attention they could provide at Dolphin Connection.

Chloe and Jenna looked up at the same time to see a tour group coming around the corner. The tour guide was just explaining that the trainers would be doing a medical demonstration with the dolphins. Chloe waved to the crowd and welcomed them to the facility. She decided to focus the med demo on the breeding practices of Atlantic Bottlenose Dolphins (ABD) since they were working with dating teenagers.

"Hi, folks! How are you doing today? Welcome to Dolphin Connection! We are so happy you came to meet our dolphin family and to learn more about marine mammals. Today, we are going to focus our medical demonstration on the breeding practices of Atlantic Bottlenose Dolphins. The four dolphins we have living in this lagoon together are Sugar & Spice and Tango & Cash. The girls are two of our teenage females — Sugar is 13 and Spice is 14. The way in which you can tell they are females is by the slits on their underside. Female dolphins have a genital slit and an anal slit that looks like a long slit and two shorter slits on the side which are mammary glands.

The slits on a female dolphin look like a division sign. Jenna will send the girls out now so you can see."

As Jenna sent the girls out to show the crowd their undersides, Chloe smiled to herself as the visitors leaned over to observe. Their faces lit up as they witnessed what had just been described. Chloe had seen this happen so many times, but it never failed to make her happy. She enjoyed seeing people taking the simple pleasure in Atlantic Bottlenose Dolphins that she did each day of her life.

As she finished her thoughts and started talking to the crowd again, the girls were just getting back to the dock for their reward.

"Now when we send out our boys, Tango & Cash, you will notice that they only have a genital slit and an anal slit. It looks like an exclamation point," Chloe continued as Jenna sent the boys for their spin around the lagoon. "Our boys are both 10 years old which makes them very ready to breed. Male dolphins usually reach sexual maturity around 8 to 10-years-old, while females are between 12 and 15. Around these ages, the dolphins move from their juvenile pods where males and females live together to separate pods (or groups of dolphins). The females live in maternity pods that include mothers and aunts, as well as young females between the ages of newborn and three-years-old. The males live in bachelor pods and often develop a strong relationship with one other male within the pod (those two may become pair-bonded, or best friends, for life). The adult males will only come into contact with the maternity pods for mating purposes. Dolphins do not live together as a family unit. Our teenagers are dating each other in hopes that they will produce some dolphin babies. Has anyone ever seen a dolphin baby?" Chloe called out to the crowd.

Nobody raised their hand.

“Well,” she replied, “you will all have to come back and see one just as soon as we have a brand-new baby dolphin. They are truly the cutest babies in the world. Though they are not newborn, we do have two, very young calves at the facility who are very unique in their own right. They are Alexa and Sophie, and they were born to the same mother on the same day. Though it is very rare, dolphins are able to have twins. Please make sure you set your eyes on these beautiful girls before you leave the facility today. Does anyone have any questions about dolphin calves in general?”

“How long is a dolphin pregnant for?” Called out one guest.

“Dolphins have a gestational period of roughly twelve to thirteen months. During that time, the mother’s belly only slightly bulges because it is important for her to stay streamlined in the water. Dolphins usually have only one calf at-a-time, for practical purposes, and the calf is born tail first. To help the mother deliver, the tail is rolled up, and the dorsal fin is folded over. The blowhole is last to emerge so that the mother can quickly push the calf to the surface to take his/her first breath. The first few years of a calf’s life are critical, and the mother will keep a close eye on them as you will see here today with our twin girls. Any more questions?”

The group was quiet, and so she proceeded with the final segment of the session.

“Before we send you all on your way, we’d like to show you one more thing that is very important for the health of our dolphins and the safety of our trainers. Our dolphins have check-ups with their veterinarians on a regular basis, just like each of you hopefully go for a yearly physical. In order to make sure the dolphins feel secure and comfortable during these exams, we practice behaviors like the tail hold which you are going to see today. Jenna is going to sit on the edge of the dock with her feet in the water and ask each dolphin, one at-a-time, to go upside down and place their tail in her lap. She will then scratch the tail with her fingernail to imitate the prick of a needle. The repetition of this process helps the dolphins feel safe when they actually have to present their tails for blood to be drawn. Tango is an expert, so he will go first, and then Cash and Sugar & Spice."

The crowd listened carefully to Chloe and watched diligently as each dolphin calmly placed its tail in Jenna's lap. They even gave the dolphins a round of applause for being such great "mock patients."

"The dolphins make much better patients than most humans I know," Chloe mused. "They definitely deserve those kudos! Thank you all for visiting with us today and for your eagerness to learn more about Atlantic Bottlenose Dolphins. All of the trainers and the beautiful grey faces around you look forward to seeing you again soon. You have been a great group."

Chloe and Jenna sent all four of the dolphins out to wave goodbye at the crowd with their pectoral fins. Then she gave Sugar & Spice and Tango & Cash each their last herring when they returned to the dock.

Chloe said goodbye to her babies, picked up her coolers and headed off the dock with Jenna. When she reached the pathway, she noticed a young man who had stayed behind and seemed to be waiting for someone.

"Chloe. Chloe Martin," he called out. "It's me! Todd Kelly from Boston College."

Chloe was shocked. She and Todd had dated during their first few years of college and then decided to go their own ways. She hadn't seen him in years.

"What are you doing here?" She blurted out before she could catch herself.

Todd smiled and laughed a little but had to understand her shock. It had been a long time and she never expected to see him again, especially here at a dolphin facility in South West Florida.

Todd had never really thought much about dolphins until he dated her, and she knew she'd really sparked his interest in marine mammals.

"I'm in town on business, saw the Dolphin Connection pamphlet in my hotel room and thought I'd stop by to see them," Todd said. "All that time we spent together really made me appreciate them. When I saw you on the dock, I couldn't believe it. I am so happy for you. You have done everything you wanted to do so badly in college. I am really proud of you. I can't think of anyone who deserves it more."

"Thanks a lot," Chloe responded. "I really appreciate your kind words. I have made a lot of sacrifices to get where I am, and sometimes I question whether it has all been worth it, but then I look out at all of those beautiful grey faces, and I know I am where I am supposed to be. Quite frankly, I never expected to see you again. I don't get up to school reunions because of my schedule, and I have fallen out of touch with most of my college friends, so I am sort of out of the loop of Boston College news. How have you been all these years?"

Todd explained that he was doing just fine and that he had moved back to New York after graduation. He had also made partner at one of the big advertising firms there. He owned a home in the suburbs and made it back to school each year for homecoming weekend and all of the reunions. He kept in touch with all of their old friends and quickly filled Chloe in on the most up-to-date gossip.

Just when Chloe started thinking to herself that she and Todd crossing paths again may be more than just a matter of coincidence, she looked down and saw a wedding ring on his finger. He must have seen the look on her face because he smiled and nodded indicating that he was indeed married.

"I ended up marrying Sheila Taggert after graduation. We started dating after you and I broke up, and it worked out because we both wanted the same things from life. I'm not sure if you knew her at B.C. or not. She was an Education Major and most of her classes were on the other side of campus."

Chloe felt as if she had been punched in the stomach. All of the things she had given up in order to work with the dolphins seemed even heavier now.

She didn't like to read the B.C. newsletter because it only reminded her of all she didn't have in her life. She purposely dropped out of touch with the people from her past, so she wouldn't have to face what they had in their lives that was missing in hers. She felt an overwhelming sadness wash over her, and she had to choke back the tears that were starting to well up in her eyes. She knew she had to pull it together just long enough to get through this conversation.

Chloe looked up and put the biggest smile on her face she could muster and cheerily said, "I am really happy for you, too. You deserve to have a wonderful family. I am sure you make a great husband and father."

Chloe didn't really know what else to say. She wanted to get back to the fish house to clean out her coolers, move on with her day and hopefully forget her encounter with Todd.

She was happy for him, but also sad for herself. She was in her early thirties now and though she had accomplished all of her professional goals, she had watched her chance of finding the right mate and settling down to have a family slip by. Seeing Todd only made it worse. She was fine as long as she didn't have to think about these things.

"Listen," she started, "I've got to get back to work. There are other dolphins waiting for me, and I have to teach a research class this afternoon to a group of our Dolphin Learner students who are here this week. It was great seeing you. I am glad you are doing so well. Please let all our old friends know that I send my regards. If anyone is ever down this way, tell them to come and see the dolphins. If you are back on business, I would be glad to set you up with a dolphin swim."

"That would be great," Todd said. "I am really glad that we ran into each other. You are an amazing person, Chloe Martin. I am just so happy that all of this worked out for you. Whatever guy is lucky enough to find you one of these days will be the luckiest man in the world. You should be proud of yourself for following your dreams and making this all happen. Whoever you share your life with should respect you for your passion and ambition. I am sorry I couldn't be that person for you."

He gave her a sweet smile, appearing to mean what he'd said.

Chloe felt sick to her stomach. She needed to say goodbye to him and get back to the routine of her day.

She leaned over and quickly gave him a hug. "Have a safe trip home. It was great seeing you and remember to let me know ahead of time if you come down again and want that dolphin swim. I've really got to get back to work. The dolphins don't wait for anyone."

It had been a bittersweet reunion, but she was glad she had run into him. He reminded her of how proud she was of herself and all she had accomplished, even if his words seemed to have an element and sound of pity to them.

As she rounded the corner at the end of the boardwalk, she saw the restroom from the night before and was reminded again of Molly's murder. Her own hurt, coupled with the grief she felt over Molly's death, was too much. She quickly made a dash for the other restrooms before the floodgates opened. She slipped into a restroom stall and had a good cry.

When she was done, she felt better and washed her face in the sink. She refocused her thoughts and vowed to look forward rather than backwards. Hope was her middle name, and she not only had hope, but faith as well. Of course, a wise young friend had once told her you needed hope in order to have faith, and her life was blessed with both.

Hope and faith sprinkled throughout a person's thoughts and actions always seemed to bring about wonderful surprises. She decided that the best place to put her energy now would be into helping find her fellow colleague's murderer. And she'd need lots of hope and faith for that task.

Chapter 10

Chloe gave herself a few minutes to regain her composure and then she left the bathroom for her office. She needed to enter the data into the computer from the training session she had just finished and then get ready to have lunch with the Dolphin Learner students and teach their research class.

She hustled back to her desk and quickly accessed the files on her computer for the dolphins with whom she had just worked. She typed in the date and time of the session, the behaviors each dolphin had completed and the type and amount of food each had eaten. Once this vital record-keeping task was completed, she began going over the file for the research class that Theresa had placed on her desk.

Chloe had observed the class a couple of times when she first interned at Dolphin Connection, but that was some time ago. It seemed, at first glance, that Molly had made some major changes to the content of the presentation. She was particularly interested in the DNA background of each dolphin, and the seminar reflected her focus.

Evidently, being a researcher had afforded her the opportunity to spend a significant amount of time enriching the seminar content by pulling new material from many resources — a luxury the trainers didn't enjoy when they could only work on their seminars between training sessions, dolphin swims and record-keeping. It was clear that she had not only expanded the scope of the seminar to make it more interesting, she had clearly tried to make it more interactive as well by offering the opportunity for students to investigate the lineage of the dolphin family at Dolphin Connection during their time at the facility.

The last revelation caused Chloe to pause. Knowing that Shannon and Theresa held certain information as confidential among staff members, it seemed unlikely either one of them would feel comfortable with the liberty Molly had taken to share sensitive material with the students.

Time was of the essence, however, and despite the red flags she discovered, which seemed to signal that something was amiss, she had to move on with her review. She had a class to teach. She spent the next half-hour going over the new material and realized it was time to leave for lunch with the students.

Her mouth watered in anticipation of the wonderful meal ahead. She loved the delectable cooking of Rose, the dorm manager. Rose and her husband Jack lived at the dorm and supervised the students who were staying there. They were a special part of Dolphin Connection and had been there even before Chloe came on board ten years prior.

Chloe relished the time she spent at the dorm with the students. She loved meeting them and hearing about all of their different backgrounds and life stories. Over the years, she had made several good friends from the groups of Dolphin Learner students. Chloe was fortunate to learn from these students as much as they learned from her.

She enjoyed the walk to the dorm because it allowed her to stroll along the path made of pavers that friends of Dolphin Connection had donated in support of the facility. She had bought several pavers herself. One in honor of all the dolphins, another for her dogs over the years (including Gabe, of course), one in thanksgiving to her grandparents for all of their love and support and another for the many colleagues she treasured at Dolphin Connection. She was thrilled each time she saw one of her special pavers and enjoyed reading the messages that other people had inscribed on their own.

The path to the dorm was also lined with hibiscus trees of many colors which seemed to be in perpetual bloom. There weren't many things in the world more beautiful to Chloe than the hibiscus blossom.

"Chloe!" Jack called as she entered the back of the dorm. "Come on in! Lunch is just getting started, and the students are eager to meet you. When Rose heard that you were coming today, she made her special burritos just for you. A shame about Molly, huh?" He leaned over and whispered to Chloe, "We were shocked when we heard the news. Things like this just don't happen around here!"

"It is quite unbelievable. It has really taken my breath away," Chloe replied. "I just hope they get to the bottom of it soon. I am the one who found her body in the bathroom stall last night, and it really freaked me out. I was even more upset when I got to work this morning and found out that Theresa and Shannon are trying to keep the whole thing quiet. I understand that they just want to protect the students and our other guests from being upset, but something doesn't feel right to me. I don't think Molly's death was an accident or the actions of a drifter. I think she was murdered. The moment I saw her body, I felt it. But here I go rambling on again. Grace had me calmed down when I talked to her last night, but I've gotten myself all worked up again. I'm sorry, Jack, please forgive me."

"Chloe, you are always free to speak your mind in my company. I just hope you aren't right about someone intentionally killing Molly. I can't imagine something like that happening here at Dolphin Connection. Hopefully, the detectives involved will do their jobs and find out what really happened, especially for Molly's sake. For now, let's leave the work to them and go inside to enjoy Rose's burritos and these new energetic students of yours."

Chloe agreed with Jack, appreciating that she could talk to him about her concerns. She took a deep breath, got her positive attitude back in place and followed him into the kitchen.

"Hi, everybody!" She called out as she entered the dorm kitchen. The students were already in line serving themselves generous portions of Rose's famous lunch.

"Hi," the group chimed back in unison.

"You must be Chloe, our trainer and teacher for this afternoon," a good looking young man called out from the front of the burrito line.

"We have been looking forward to meeting you," another woman turned and announced to Chloe.

"We have heard that you are the best trainer around these parts," an older woman with a Texas accent joked with her.

"That's quite a reputation to have to live up to," Chloe said and smiled back at the woman.

"Oh, don't worry," the woman called over, "there is no pressure or anything. We just expect you to make us all into perfect dolphin trainers by the end of the week."

"Well," said Chloe, "since there is no such thing as a perfect dolphin trainer, I guess I don't have to worry. If the dolphins think we are getting anywhere close to perfect, they get out of line just to shake things up and put us back in our place. In the end, we are only as perfect as they let us be."

"Isn't that the truth," Rose agreed, a longtime dolphin handler herself. "I have been humbled more by those beautiful animals than any other creature on Earth, and I don't get to spend half as much time working with our dolphin family and doing public sessions like their trainers do each day."

Rose's comments started a discussion about the differences between a trainer and a handler. Chloe went through the buffet line as she tried to explain the two positions to the students. It was a difficult concept for most people to understand because the majority of facilities only use trainers.

Dolphin Connection was proud of the fact that they encouraged intimate contact between much of their staff and their dolphin family by offering opportunities such as being a handler, someone who gives the dolphins signals and feeds them, but leaves training new behaviors and working with them in public swim sessions to the trainers. Some of the students were excited to hear that there was a possibility of working closely with the dolphins without actually having to be a trainer.

Lunch finished quickly with engaging conversation and Chloe enjoyed herself immensely. She even managed to forget about the previous night's events. Her presentation of the Research Seminar went more smoothly than she had anticipated. Molly had made important changes to the curriculum which made the class much more interesting for the students.

When the seminar concluded, Chloe gave the students instructions to gather their things and follow her for a tour of the facility. She absolutely loved introducing the new students to the dolphins and teaching them little tricks to tell the dolphins apart.

"Grab your binders, a pen, a hat and some sun block, and you guys should be all set. A bottle of water is always a good idea in this heat, too!"

“Shall we bring our swim suits just in case?” One of the students jokingly asked.

“Not just yet, though I know you are all super eager to get in the water and have your dolphin swims. It is an unbelievable part of your stay here this week. Just don’t wish it to come too fast, because then you’ll be sad it’s over.”

“Very true,” Rose agreed as she listened-in from the kitchen.

“Now, grab your stuff and let’s get out there. I can’t wait for you all to meet our dolphin family.”

The group walked quickly from the dorm over to the dolphin lagoons and talked amongst themselves of their personal dreams. When they reached the first lagoon, Chloe gave them an overview on dolphin etiquette.

“Remember, we are the visitors to their home, and we must be respectful. We always want the dolphins to feel secure and comfortable, and we certainly want them to be happy to see us.”

As if on cue, Trixie, one of the oldest and most athletic dolphins, started to speed around the lagoon and stopped in front of Chloe and the group to make her presence known. She popped out of the water, splashed like crazy with her pectoral fins and squeaked and squealed in delight. The students went wild, of course. Their joy could be felt as if a shot of electricity had run through the crowd.

Chloe introduced Trixie and pointed out some characteristics that would help everyone tell her apart from the rest of the dolphins, “Trixie is our movie star here at Dolphin Connection. She has appeared in several commercials, TV shows and even on the big screen. Chances are, if you have seen a dolphin performing in one type of film media or another, it was probably Trixie. She is a particularly large dolphin, and she can perform amazing aerials. Her size makes her light up as a real presence on the big screen. She tends to let out a big scream when she does her flip-and-a-half which captures the attention of everyone in earshot. Chances are, you'll never have a problem identifying her…she will definitely let you know it is her!"

"Chloe, is Trixie big in general or just big for a female?" One of the younger students queried.

"With dolphins, in relation to size, it is similar to humans. Males and females vary in size according to their genetic history. Trixie's parents were big, and so she is big! Alan, who is sharing a lagoon with Trixie at the moment, is a small male because both of his parents were small. Good question! I'm glad you brought it up! Let's move onto the next lagoon and see who else is waiting for us!"

Chloe led the students down the narrow boardwalk that surrounded each of the lagoons and opened the gate which kept the dolphin areas secure from the general visitors for their own safety as well as the safety of the dolphins. She asked the last student in line to secure the gate before moving on. It never ceased to amaze her how visitors would go right onto the boardwalks if the gates were not properly secured despite the signs asking them not to do so.

When everyone had safely filed onto the girls' docks, Chloe introduced the students to her closest dolphin friends in the world — Cali, Emma, Alexa and Sophie. The bond that Chloe shared with these four dolphins was beyond words. Being in their presence made chills run down her spine and her heart overflow with deep gratitude.

"Of course, it is easy to tell who's who in this lagoon! We have two mature females. The new Mommy, Cali, and the Aunt, Emma. It is normal for females in the wild to support one another when new calves are born. It is especially helpful in this case since Cali had twins to care for around the clock."

"Is it common for dolphins to have twins?" Asked one of the students.

"Not at all," responded Chloe. "We are very fortunate that both Alexa and Sophie have done so well. It is especially challenging for dolphins to sustain a twin pregnancy in the wild because it affects their ability to stay safe from predators like sharks. Remember, it's the streamlined shape of the dolphin's body that helps them move through the water so freely and gracefully. Carrying two calves doesn't do much for that streamline. The other challenge is during the birth process itself because dolphins must surface to take a breath soon after being born so that they won't drown. The mother will often push the calf to the surface. When there is another calf waiting to be born, this complicates matters. Fortunately, dolphins are born tail first so that the blow hole does not get exposed to the open water prematurely in the delivery process. Cali handled the delivery like a pro. She is a very protective Mom. She nurses both of the girls and keeps them close by her side. Emma stays on top of the girls, too, and makes sure they don't come too close to the dock yet. We are excited to get to know them better when they start getting involved in the training sessions."

"How in the world do you tell the calves apart?" A student with a recognizable NY accent blurted out.

"It isn't easy, at all. Right now, Alexa is slightly larger than Sophie and her dorsal fin has a more distinct curve to it at the top. As they grow and mature, more differences will emerge. It is pretty easy to identify Cali and Emma. As long as you can see Cali's tail flukes, you are golden. She has a beautiful circle in her right fluke that was caused by a bacterial infection she had years ago. Unfortunately, the infection ate right through her skin and left permanent damage, but luckily it left a beautiful circular mark. When she waves her tail flukes, there is something about it that is perfectly magical. It is quite easy to spot Emma as well, especially now that she is in with the calves. Emma is very large, the largest female here, and she is in her late 40's. Over the years, some of the skin around her rostrum has been worn away from use, not surprisingly since dolphins explore their worlds with their rostrums, and now she looks like she has a white beard from the scar tissue. Also, you'll always find her close to one of the calves. These girls have their own maternity pod here, and Emma takes her 'Auntie' role very seriously."

"You mentioned that Emma is in her forties. Has she ever had a calf of her own?" Interjected one of the students.

"We do believe that Emma is in her late forties. She came to us from another facility which had collected her from the wild as a calf while it was still legal. Dolphins in human care can actually live a great deal longer (up to 40 or 50) than those in the wild (which average around 25). Emma has never had a calf of her own, which is very sad because she enjoys being a mother so much."

"How come you have never mated her?" Asked another one of the curious students.

"We have tried many times, with no success. With dolphins, it is like it is with humans. Some of them just don't get pregnant for many different reasons, even with the modern-day assistance of artificial insemination, which we have tried with Emma. For whatever reason, she never became a mother herself. But she sure loves helping raise the calves in her maternity pod!"

The students took a few extra minutes admiring the calves, as everyone does. Chloe was touched by their enthusiasm and excitement. After a while, she called to them to follow her to the boys' lagoon.

"This way," she directed as everyone followed her to the last lagoon which was beautifully situated on the Gulf of Mexico. "We're going to say hello now to our wild and crazy teenage boys."

As the group approached, Tango & Cash went wild. They sped around their lagoon chasing each other until they tired themselves out. They finally stopped to check out the interested students. Chloe knelt on the floating dock and leaned over to hug and kiss each of the boys. They knew she didn't have any fish, but they wanted the interaction nonetheless.

"These boys are so energetic, it will be hard to catch them in a slow moment so that you can tell them apart. Tango has two small notches in his dorsal fin, and he is quite larger than Cash. These two males have become what we call 'pair-bonded', and in the wild, as they grow older, they would live together in a bachelor pod. Sexually-mature male dolphins live together in a group and will impregnate females in a maternity pod when they cross paths. The mature males do not stay with the females, however, and they do not stay with the young. And hold all jokes about that situation, please. We've heard them all."

The students laughed quietly, although with a loving-kind understanding, and quickly focused their attention on the playful males in front of them. Tango and then Cash found some seaweed which they proceeded to toss (by using the ends of their rostrums) at the students. It took the students by surprise and landed on the head of one of the young ladies. Everyone burst out in laughter, including Chloe.

"Go ahead and throw it back, Lynn," Chloe told the now wet dolphin enthusiast. "The boys are in the mood to play."

This brought about a fantastic game of "seaweed toss" that brought smiles a mile-wide to the faces of the students. Chloe thought to herself, as she did each day, that she had the best job in the world.

"Go ahead and keep that piece of seaweed for your scrapbook, Lynn, since you were the first hit, and then we'll move onto the next lagoon."

The students were sad to leave Tango & Cash, but after a long game with them, the boys had begun chasing each other around the lagoon once more. Chloe led the students to a lagoon across the way which was rather large and had a beautiful expanse of the open Gulf behind it.

"This lagoon works really well if we need to shoot a commercial or a part for a movie. It works nicely because it's so big, and there are no buildings from the facility that can be seen, not even any of the homes along the coast from this angle. Right now, we have a few of our 'golden girls' living together in this lagoon, enjoying the open space. Ernestine is easy to spot because of the scar that is visible on her back. We believe she was attacked by a shark in the wild when she was young as the scar closely resembles the jaws of a shark. She is a sweet, strong dolphin in her mature years. She has slowed down some, but she still loves her training sessions. One of her lagoon mates is Keira, a retiree of the US Naval Research Program. You can read about Keira in many dolphin books as she had a very successful Navy career. She was collected from the wild as a young calf and trained by the Navy to locate bombs and other devices that were hidden underwater by our enemies. Keira and other marine mammals help greatly to keep our underwater military personnel safe, and yes, the safety of the marine mammals involved in these operations is of the utmost importance. Keira worked hard for many years, and she is easy to spot from the various markings of scar tissue that cover her body. Keira came to live out the rest of her life in a comfortable, supportive environment and to get lots of TLC."

"Who is the third dolphin in the lagoon? She looks so small. And her skin is perfect without any scars at all. Is she also older?" Lynn, who was now drenched from the seaweed toss with the boys, wondered out loud.

"She sure is. That is our Persephone. She isn't quite as old as the other girls, but she has some GI health issues and likes their slower pace. Persy, as we call her for short, enjoys looking beautiful. She doesn't let any of the other dolphins 'rake' or drag their teeth across her body in a playful manner. You'd be hard pressed to find a scar anywhere on her. She is what we humans refer to as a diva or a princess. When we throw new toys in the lagoons for the dolphins, Persy likes to use them to dress up. You might walk by and find her with a scarf draped over her and ring toys like bracelets on her pectoral fins. Persy is a real character. She is the mother of Cash who we met a little earlier. Her pregnancy with Cash was not an easy one and it took a real toll on her health. We often have to 'catch' her, place her on a stretcher and administer medication through a tube to help calm her stomach condition. We love our beautiful Persy and try to keep her as healthy and as happy as possible."

"Dolphins are very similar to humans in many ways," a student commented.

"They sure are," Chloe agreed. "And you become just as attached, that's for sure. These dolphins are my extended family," she explained and knew that many of the students would feel the same way by the time they went home.

Chloe finished introducing the students to the rest of the dolphins and thoroughly enjoyed the experience. She showed the students where each of the departments was located, the restroom facilities, the gift shop and the fish house. Fortunately, there were volunteers working in the fish house, and the students were able to see them in action checking each of the fish thoroughly, cleaning them and assembling specified coolers for each of the dolphins with the right type and amount (weight) of fish.

"Look over here, everyone. This is where the finished coolers are stored and are ready to be picked up by a trainer for their next session. When each of the trainers finish a session, they bring back the cooler and clean it out so that it will be ready to be filled once again. Our dolphins eat restaurant-quality fish and receive vitamin supplements as well. Their diet is crucial to their health and well-being. A dolphin receives all of their moisture through the fish they eat, so a well-fed dolphin is also a well- hydrated dolphin. When dolphins like Persy stop eating because of stomach issues, they can become dehydrated quickly. The work of the volunteers in this room is critical to the operation of the facility and the welfare of the dolphins. If any of you decide to come back to Dolphin Connection and volunteer or intern, you will most definitely spend time in this room. But don't worry. The hours you spend in the fish house will be some of the most memorable you spend here. We all bond in this place. It happens when you stink like fish and are covered all over in tiny scales."

The volunteers in the room who ranged in age from their teens to their 70's laughed and nodded in agreement. Chloe thanked all of them for their hard work and led the students outside. She had them dip the bottom of their shoes in the tray filled with bleach water - as they had on their way in - keeping germs from spreading into or out of the fish house.

"If you think that looks like hard work, wait until you have to shovel sea grass out of the lagoons like those volunteers over there." Chloe pointed to three young women in their 20's or so who were scooping heavy piles of sea grass out of one of the lagoons in the hot afternoon sun. "Now that is hard work, but also lots of fun as you can see!"

One of the volunteers had fallen into a pile of the sea grass, and she and the other two were hysterical laughing.

"The friendships you make here often last a lifetime," Chloe mentioned, grateful for every single one she'd made there.

The energy and interest amongst the students was contagious, and Chloe soaked it all in. She guided the students past the tiki hut that offered drinks and snacks for the visitors to the facility. Then she brought them over to the trainer's office which was the golden palace for most of them — the place they wanted to reach since they were young children and first fell in love with dolphins. Many of the students' eyes widened and then froze in place when Chloe motioned them inside.

"It's okay, come on in," she beckoned them. "The other trainers won't bite."

As always, the students were nervous but in total awe as they stepped inside the trainer's office.

The trainers in the office waved and greeted them and made them feel at ease. Chloe explained briefly "a day in the life of a trainer," hoping to inspire the students further and end on a high note before she led them back to the dorm.

"Hope you all had a great afternoon! Now, I better get you back to the dorm because I know Rose will have something wonderful for dinner prepared for you soon. Thanks for making it an extraordinary time for me."

Chloe hugged each of the students and promised to check in with them during their week-long stay at Dolphin Connection.

Chapter 11

After her time with the students, Chloe's afternoon progressed smoothly. She remained in a good mood the rest of the day and agreed to an invitation from one of her friends to go to their favorite restaurant — The Hurricane — that evening for dinner.

"Take care, everyone. I'll see you tomorrow," Chloe called as she left the trainer's office at 5:30 PM. "I'll meet you at The Hurricane at 7PM," she reminded her friend Bailey as she slipped out the door.

"Eliza can't make it, so it will just be the two of us," Bailey called out in return.

Because it gave her extra time with the dolphins, Chloe usually preferred to stay late and closedown the facility. Due to the stress from her discovery of Molly's body the evening before, she had jumped at the opportunity to leave early when the offer was made by Theresa.

She drove home quickly, in New York fashion, and immediately took Gabe out for his walk. They made a loop around the neighborhood, and then he started pulling towards home for dinner. Chloe fed him, hopped in the shower and changed into clothes that were appropriate for a night out in Southern Florida.

She loved that she had kept herself in shape and still looked as good in her early thirties as she had in college. She dressed in a pretty pink, sleeveless shirt that had a scalloped neck and a khaki skirt. She reached for a pair of open-toed sandals and was thankful she had recently painted her toes "perky pink." When she took the time to style and blow it out, the hi-lights she had done really showed up in her shoulder-length, brown hair. To finish off her look, she put on her favorite diamond "snuggly" hoop earrings and slipped her watch onto her wrist. She was ready to go just in time. She gave Gabe a quick hug and kiss and headed out the door.

She arrived at The Hurricane a few minutes before Bailey and scouted out a good table. The restaurant was a favorite of the locals, and it often became crowded. As Chloe waited for her friend, she glanced around to see if there was anyone in the place she knew.

When she spotted Todd at a nearby table with several other men and a very attractive young lady, she couldn't believe her eyes. They had several pitchers of beer and things seemed to be getting quite lively. If Chloe weren't mistaken, it seemed as if Todd was hitting on the lady in the group. Surely not, she thought, remembering how emphatic Todd had been about his wonderful family and perfect life.

"What are you thinking about?" Bailey asked as she slipped into the booth across from Chloe.

"Hey, Bailey," Chloe responded. "You startled me. I was just thinking about somebody I saw today at work who is now sitting with that rowdy group at the table across the way."

"Anyone important?" Bailey asked as she picked up her menu and began to scan through it, an action that was totally unnecessary since both of them ordered the same thing every time they ate at The Hurricane.

"Just someone from my past," Chloe replied. "He used to be very important to me. But he is nothing anymore."

"Are you sure about that?" Bailey asked. "Old flames can be very hard to get over, especially when you see one unexpectedly on your own turf."

"What do you mean by that, on my own turf?" Chloe asked sort of defensively. "I'd be over him if I saw him in New England, New York or right here in Florida. The past is the past, and my past with him ended a long time ago. No regrets here, especially now that I've seen him flirting with another woman while his wife and kids are at home up North not knowing their perfect world isn't quite so perfect."

"Ouch!" Bailey exclaimed and put her hands up in the air, signaling she was sorry she brought it up. "It sounds like you are still hanging onto some of the hurt or the anger or both."

"I was before today," Chloe responded, feeling bad for snapping at her friend. "For years, I held onto the pain I felt when Todd told me we had no future. Even this morning, I crumbled into tears after I finished talking to him. But I had a really good time with the students, and I did a great job presenting the Research Class. I had a successful training session with the girls this afternoon and then went home to my beautiful apartment that overlooks the Gulf of Mexico and was greeted by the best dog in the world. I'm here tonight with a terrific friend about to have my favorite seafood dinner. If my life with Todd had continued, I'd be the wife with the kids up in NY who has no idea her husband is flirting with some woman ten years his junior while on a business trip in Florida. I feel better about the situation than I have in years. I believe I have finally let it go. But enough of that, I'm starving and just want to enjoy my favorite meal and relax with my good friend. I am still feeling the stress from last evening and just want to unwind."

"I agree. Let's leave it at that and move on. I heard through the grapevine that you were the one who found Molly's body. Go figure…you finding a body again, but so close to home this time. Tell me all the details of what happened. I couldn't gather much at all at work today. It seemed as if Shannon and Theresa wanted to make the whole thing just disappear. I don't understand that at all. Molly was a kind, intelligent woman who worked very hard for Dolphin Connection. She deserves more than the attention she received today."

"My thoughts exactly," Chloe agreed. "I just don't understand it. A murder took place on their property of one of their employees and they have basically made the subject taboo. It just doesn't seem right. I know that their priority is the dolphins, above everything else, but this seems like an exceptional situation. My only hope is that the Police give the matter the appropriate attention. I met with the detectives last night, and they seem very capable. A little afraid of the dolphins and our floating docks, but capable as detectives, none the less," Chloe smirked to herself as she recalled Detective White's near fall into the dolphin lagoon.

"What was that smile for?" Bailey asked, evidently noticing the sheepish grin on Chloe's face. "If I didn't know better, I'd think you met the love of your life last night."

"Well, he was pretty incredible," Chloe admitted. "I was so shook up about finding Molly's body that I was really surprised I could even notice how great he was. I felt pretty guilty about it, at the time, too. I mean there was Molly's body in the bathroom stall, a stone's throw away, and I couldn't get over how fantastic the detective was who was sent to investigate her death. I am a rotten person, for sure. And the worst part of it is that I will probably never see him again in my life. I signed a statement last night, and they interviewed me for quite some time until Theresa arrived on the scene. Oh well! Trusting in faith, my heart knows we'll cross paths again somehow…if it is meant to be."

"You never know what lies ahead," Bailey replied. "And don't worry about your feelings of attraction. I'm sure Molly understood. As a woman, she would have known how rare it is to find a potentially amazing man. It's not like you jumped his bones there on the dock, did you?"

"Very funny," Chloe retorted. "I was very professional, of course. I mean he was interviewing me as part of a murder investigation! That said, I couldn't get past this tingly feeling I had inside when I was talking with him. But enough of that, let's get John over here so that we can order. I can't wait any longer. Every time he goes by, we are chatting, and he waves to let us know that he is ready when we are."

John, a Florida local and longtime waiter at The Hurricane, knew Chloe and Bailey well enough to leave them alone when they were engrossed in conversation. Long ago, when the girls had first started visiting the restaurant, he used to stop by constantly to see if they were ready to order, but he was always delayed because they were in the midst of a conversation. Since then, he'd learned that it was much easier to have them signal him when they were ready.

Actually, he could have gone ahead and placed their order. They always got the same thing every time they came in, but he went through the process of checking in with them, more as a formality than anything else.

Chloe and Bailey enjoyed their fruity cocktails, Malibu and pineapple, a fitting drink for their tropical Florida climate, and then continued to talk over dinner. They each had the seared tuna for an appetizer, made to perfection as always, and then the stone crabs for dinner.

As they enjoyed their food, Chloe recounted the events of the previous evening for Bailey. She knew she could trust Bailey. They had been friends for a long time, and she was much more mature than some of the other younger trainers. And they both knew that while Chloe had no formal training in crime investigation, her careful observations and attention to her feelings and intuition had helped her solve a few challenging cases in the past.

They topped off dinner with key lime pie and decided to call it a night. They said their goodbyes, and Chloe ducked into the girl's room one last time before she headed home. She knew Gabe would want to go for a walk right away, and she had a better chance of visiting the bathroom here alone than she did at home when greeted by her persuasive poodle who always seemed to get his way.

She passed through the crowded bar area on her way to the front door and accidentally bumped into a man as she tried to pass.

"Excuse me," she murmured as she continued to move ahead.

"No problem at all," the gentleman responded.

Chloe recognized the voice from somewhere, although she wasn't quite sure from where, so she turned back to see if she knew the person it belonged to. She ended up looking right into the beautiful eyes of Detective White.

Talk about shocked…

Chapter 12

"Hi! Funny meeting you here. I'm Chloe," she stated as she reached out her hand in greeting to Detective White. "We met last night at Dolphin Connection."

"I know exactly who you are," Detective White responded as he reached out his hand to meet hers. "I have a pretty sharp memory for details. I guess that's what makes me a good detective."

Chloe laughed to herself, feeling silly. Of course, he remembered who she was. It was his job to remember her, though she couldn't help thinking there'd been a spark when she'd turned around and their eyes connected. Maybe even distant bells ringing…

What a ridiculous thought, she chided herself. Nobody sees fireworks or hears wedding bells when they meet the love of their life, right? At least it had never happened to her...till now.

"Are you on your way out?" Detective White asked, bringing Chloe somewhat back to her senses.

"Yes, I just finished up dinner with my friend Bailey and I am heading home to take care of my dog," she replied, trying to sound calm despite the butterflies fluttering in a complete frenzy in her stomach.

"Do you have time to stay for a drink with me?" He asked and flashed a gorgeous grin, dimples and all, a smile Chloe couldn't refuse.

“Sure. I guess Gabe wouldn’t mind if I’m out just a bit longer.”

“I sure hope Gabe is your dog and not a significant other,” Detective White jokingly said.

“Yes, he’s my mini poodle. I’m a poodle person. I’ve had a poodle in my life since I was three-years-old. I adore all dogs, but poodles are my breed. They are incredibly intelligent, loyal, affectionate and just plain fun. They are characters to the core. Gabe is an awesome dog, but then again all my dogs have been awesome.”

“I could tell when we talked last night that you are a real animal person. Your passion for the dolphins and their welfare amazed me, so it comes as no surprise that you love dogs, too. I hope I get to meet Gabe sometime. I grew up with dogs, but since I have been out on my own, I haven’t had an animal because I’m not home enough to take care of one. I miss the companionship I shared with my dogs growing up.”

“I don’t know what I’d do without Gabe,” Chloe sighed. “I understand what you mean about the time constraints of your job, though. I often wish I had more time at home just to hang out with Gabe. I’m sure he would love to meet you. He’s a big guy fan. He likes to play rough with his toys and get wound up.”

“I look forward to meeting him,” Detective White said and seemed to genuinely mean it. “Now why don’t I get us a couple of drinks so that I don’t further delay your arrival home? I am sure he’s anxious to get out for a walk. What can I get you?”

“I’ll take a virgin pina colada, and thanks for being so considerate about me needing to get home. Most guys don’t understand planning life around a dog.”

“Let’s make it Brian, and no problem at all. I respect your relationship with Gabe. I can tell you are a good

Mom." With another wicked smile, Brian turned and went to the bar to retrieve their drinks.

Chloe couldn't believe what had just happened. One moment she was heading for the door of the restaurant after a really nice and satisfying evening with her friend, and the next thing she knows, she's bumping into Detective White. No…Brian…she corrected herself.

They were talking with an ease and comfort she had not shared with a man in she couldn't remember how long. She wanted to pinch herself to make sure she wasn't dreaming. He seemed too good to be true — handsome, professional, polite, respectful, and a fellow dog lover to boot. Don't get too excited, she reminded herself. This is not normal.

You never know what is beneath the surface, she reminded herself. She had just met him the night before and really knew nothing about his background. Even so, she couldn't help but be a little excited. It had been quite some time since a man even interested her.

"Here is your drink, Chloe. Did I wake you from a dream?" He asked as he passed her a cocktail. "You looked like you were far off in another world for a moment there."

"Oh no," she blurted out in embarrassment, reaching for her drink, wondering if he knew she was thinking of him. "I was just thinking about all the work I have to do tomorrow," she offered, hoping that her little white lie sounded believable.

She certainly couldn't tell him she was wondering if he was the man of her dreams. She laughed to herself at the idea of sharing that kind of thought with a man she had just met. It was certain to make him run for the door and never look back.

If she knew one thing, it was that men liked to take things slowly and really get to know a woman before the prospects of marriage and children ever entered their minds. On this point, however, it certainly would make life easier if men and women thought more alike.

Chloe considered her thought process similar to many other women. Lots of women thought about whether or not the man they were interested in would make a great husband and father. If a man was way off the mark, why waste either of their time? A pretty logical and reasonable way to think, but not necessarily one agreed upon by many men she knew.

She had discussed the topic with many of her male friends, and they thought her way of thinking was crazy and unfair. They felt there was no need to even think about such serious things when they first met a woman. Why not just hang out and enjoy the time together, they argued.

Not everyone has to be a potential marriage partner and the father of your children, her best friend Paul would tease. Dating is a lot more fun if you just let things happen…or not, he explained. But that is not a possibility for most women, Chloe replied, and then she would launch into one of her *Men are From Mars and Women From Venus* talks. No matter how many times they had the conversation, Paul would never agree with her argument that men and women are just wired differently, and neither could change when it came to major matters of the heart. They usually ended up agreeing to disagree.

"There you go…off in dream land again," Brian teased as Chloe realized that she had been thinking to herself for a moment too long.

"Sorry," she responded. "You have my full attention now. So, I hope you have something really important to say," she poked fun back at him.

Brian smiled and thought to himself that he was amazed how comfortable he felt with Chloe. She was pretty, smart, athletic and outgoing. Her love for the dolphins and for her dog were commendable.

"She would make a wonderful wife," he heard his mother whispering in his ear. "Don't let this one get away," her voice continued.

Brian smiled to himself. This time, his mother may be right. Chloe seemed almost too good to be true.

"It looks like I've caught you daydreaming now," Chloe joked as she gently shook Brian's bicep, amazed at the warmth she felt from simply touching his body.

"You are right. I was just thinking about how amazing you are, and how happy I am that we bumped into each other tonight."

Chloe was blown away. She couldn't believe her ears. This guy really was too good to be true. It all seemed so magical, especially considering the fact they had initially met because of a murder investigation and had stumbled into each other just a couple hours after she had finally closed the door on all of the hurt Todd had caused in her past.

"Wow!" Chloe exclaimed. "That is about the nicest thing a guy has ever said to me. I was thinking the very same thing about you just a few minutes ago."

"I'm glad to hear it," replied Brian. "Or else I'd be standing here feeling like a jerk right about now."

"I'm really glad we met up tonight," Chloe went on. "It was very unexpected, but really nice. I better get going, though, before Gabe gets upset with me. He is overdue for his late-night walk and treat."

"I hope I haven't held you up too long," Brian said sincerely. "Maybe we could get together for dinner tomorrow night, after we both get home from work."

“That sounds great. I’ve been dying to try that new Italian restaurant on Main Street. How does that sound to you?” She asked.

“Sounds perfect! I love Italian food, and I’ve heard from some people at the station that the restaurant is authentic. Does 7:30 sound okay to you?”

“I’ll see you there. And by the way, I’m not sure if I should be asking you this or not, but have you been able to make any sense of Molly’s murder?”

“We’re obviously in the preliminary part of our investigation, and we spent the whole day collecting evidence. Waiting for the autopsy report from the Coroner’s Office now. At this point, we’ve got more questions than answers. A restroom is a very public place and makes fingerprint identification very hard for us. How are you doing, by the way? You were pretty shaken up last night when we talked.”

“Well, because of the support of some good friends, a productive day with the dolphins and some new students that have come to study at Dolphin Connection this week, I am doing a lot better today than I was last night. Something did bother me today, though,” Chloe hesitated before she went on.

“Is it something you feel comfortable sharing with me?” Brian sensitively prodded.

He sounded as if he didn’t want to seem pushy, but at the same time, was eager to gather any information that might help him solve the case.

“Well, it was just a little strange at work today because Theresa and Shannon put out a very terse memo about what happened last night and requested that nobody talk about the situation while at Dolphin Connection. They stated they felt it was important for the guests who traveled from great distances to be with us not to be upset by the murder and that the dolphins not be exposed to any additional trauma than they were last evening when all of you came onto the property at a time of the night when they are supposed to have private 'dolphin time' away from all human beings. I mean, I understand their concern for both the guests and especially for the dolphins, but one of their employees was murdered…on their property! I just think they could have shown a little more sympathy for Molly and her family. The memo seemed almost cold, rather than compassionate. I guess it rubbed me the wrong way, that's all. It just furthered my gut instinct that Molly's murder could possibly be personal."

"Never underestimate your gut instinct about something. Often times, it proves to be right," Brian offered. "If you felt something was off today with the way in which the Directors handled the situation, then it's pertinent to our investigation. You never know. I've learned over the years to take nothing for granted when it comes to trying to solve a crime. The smallest details can often point you in the right direction. Feel this one out over your next few days at work. Maybe Shannon and Theresa rushed when they wrote up that memo because they were pressed for time. Theresa stayed through the night to make sure that everything went smoothly with the CSI and that the dolphins were handling the invasion of their space okay. She was very up front in our interviews and very helpful with the team. She was adamant that Dolphin Connection be open to the public this morning so that nobody would have to miss their dolphin swims. She explained to us how people planned their trips and booked reservations to get in the water and swim with the dolphins, months ahead of time. She seemed genuinely concerned that nobody be disappointed and that the dolphins return to their regular schedule. If we need to do any further investigative work on the grounds, she is going to coordinate a schedule with us. I hope that makes you feel a little better about the situation."

"You are right. Theresa was probably just thinking about how to keep the guests happy, the dolphins healthy and her staff calm. She is a true businesswoman and handles stressful situations everyday of her life. If she had become all emotional about Molly's death, then everybody would have become emotional as well and the whole staff would have suffered a meltdown. Shannon and Theresa kept things running smoothly today, and for that, I am grateful. You make a lot of sense, Brian. I guess that is why you are the detective, and I am the dolphin trainer."

"I guess so," Brian agreed as he gave Chloe a reassuring rub on her back. A rub that sent chills of excitement up and down her spine.

"Let me walk you to your car so you can get home," he offered.

"That would be great. Do you have to say goodbye to your friends first?"

"I'll come back in to see them. I don't want to delay you any longer. Gabe might hold it against me!"

Chapter 13

After sending Chloe on her way, Detective White briefly spoke with the friends he was with at The Hurricane and then headed for his car.

He had recently bought a new, red, Jeep Grand Cherokee, and he still enjoyed the "new car" smell and feel of it.

He took the scenic route home and put the windows down to enjoy the ocean breeze. His head was still spinning from the night's events. He couldn't believe he had bumped into Chloe at the bar. He had been amazed the night before, so taken with her. Usually, he barely noticed someone when he interviewed them during an investigation except to make sure he helped them remember all the pertinent information relevant to the case.

He smiled as he thought about the dinner he had set up with her for the next evening. It had been a long while since he had been interested in asking a woman out for a date. He was starting to think he would never meet anyone again.

He kept busy enough with his job, and when he had time, with his hobbies as well, but they certainly didn't replace the feeling of sharing his life with somebody. His golf clubs didn't keep him warm at night, and the fish he loved to admire while scuba diving didn't go home with him.

He tried not to think about it too much, but his mother never forgot to remind him when they spoke. He knew she was just concerned about him, but having her go at him really didn't help matters at all.

On the way home, he decided to turn off on Ocean Avenue and take a walk on the pier. He parked the Jeep in the lot closest to the pier, got out and locked the car.

He liked to come to the pier late at night when it was quiet. At sunset, it was a popular place for both locals and tourists, and you could never find a convenient parking spot. If he had friends or family in town for a visit, he always brought them to see the spectacular sunset the view from the pier offered, but otherwise, he avoided the place at all costs during peak hours. He knew it was a great place to see wild dolphins during the early morning and twilight hours, when they fed on the schools of fish, and wondered if Chloe ever came this way to see them.

He walked straight to the end of the pier and leaned against the railing. He could hear the rustling of the palm trees that lined the beach and the crash of the waves against the shore. He closed his eyes and soaked up the smell of the fresh air and the sounds of the southern Florida coast.

He had decided long ago that he would always live in this part of the country. He loved everything about Florida. The warm weather, the radiant sunshine, the friendly people, the lush vegetation and the abundant marine life. It was perfect for him, and he thanked God for it every morning when he took his three-mile jog on the beach. He simply couldn't imagine living anywhere else despite the pleas that came from his family back in Connecticut. He left the Northeast once and for all eight years ago, and he never planned on looking back.

He wished he could see his parents and his nieces and nephews more often, but still, Florida was his home, and he didn't want to leave. When he visited with his family, he simply made sure he emphasized quality over quantity time.

The nice thing about being so far away was that he could go out with Chloe the next evening and his mother would be none the wiser. That way, if things didn't work out, she wouldn't get her hopes up and give him the third degree about what went wrong.

He took one last, deep breath, soaking up all the energy he could from his beautiful surroundings. It was getting late, and he wanted to get to bed so he would be ready to go in the morning. It was crucial to find any leads in a potential murder investigation in the hours closest to when it may have occurred, and the clock had already been ticking for over 24 hours now.

Brian was passionate about all his cases, but this one seemed to be even more critical. He had made a promise to Chloe that he would do his very best to track down Molly's killer, and he intended to keep his promise.

He always kept his promises. He just wished other people kept theirs, too. Maybe this time would be different.

Chapter 14

Chloe rushed out the door and jumped into her car. She loved to drive her Mustang GT Convertible with the top down, soaking in the intoxicating rays of the Florida sunshine. She had left work right on time, sped home to take care of Gabe and showered and changed into appropriate clothes for her date with Brian.

The latter took quite some time, despite the fact that she had chosen what she was going to wear the previous evening after she arrived home from The Hurricane. She'd changed her mind several times, however, and tried on three other outfits.

In the end, she stuck with her original choice — a Lily Pulitzer ensemble that consisted of a pink skirt with palm trees, a matching lime green t-shirt with a subtle palm in the lower left corner and a pink sweater that she tied around her shoulders. It was too hot tonight to wear it, but it completed the outfit. She looked very Floridian, not too conservative or too sexy, just classy in a mature way.

Before she left, she received good luck kisses from Gabe and told him how sorry she was to be going out two nights in a row. She told him she would make it up to him with a long walk on the beach the following morning. It was her day off, and she planned to spend it at home with Gabe taking care of all the housework that had piled up while she was at work all week.

After putting the roof up on her car so that her hair wouldn't get windblown, she drove by Dolphin Connection on the way to dinner and waved a silent hello to the dolphins. During their play session earlier in the day, she had told her dolphin girlfriends all about her date tonight.

She loved to talk to them about everything that was going on in her life. They were great listeners and certainly excellent secret keepers. They seemed to enjoy the long conversations she had with them, and they never took off when she was in the middle of talking. It amazed her how they would always wait until she had finished her thoughts, kissed them on top of the rostrum to say thank you for listening and given them a big hug before they would go off to swim around their lagoon.

Gabe was the same way at home. He always gave her his full attention, whether she was happy, sad, sick or tired, and he always forgave her no matter what the circumstances. He, like the dolphins, loved her unconditionally. Tears came to her eyes just thinking about how blessed she had been with all the animals who graced her life.

She stopped herself from getting too sentimental because she had tears forming in her eyes and she didn't want to mess up the make-up she had so carefully applied a half hour earlier. She had jammed her tube of pink lipstick in her purse, but she didn't have room for all of her other beauty supplies. She needed her eye make-up to last throughout the evening.

She pulled the Mustang into a spot she found behind the restaurant, locked the car and hurried to the front door. She made it just in the nick of time. She often pushed it so that she would barely make it to a social event on time, preferring not to be the first one there, but she didn't want to be late for her first date with Brian. She reached the front door of the restaurant at the same time he did.

He had been lucky enough to find a parking spot right out front on Main Street and seemed pleased to see that she hadn't been sitting and waiting for him. He greeted her with a kiss on the cheek and opened the door for her to enter the busy establishment.

They were both greeted with the wonderful smell of garlic and a friendly hostess who asked for their name. Brian gave the hostess his last name, and they were quickly seated. As they made their way to their table, Chloe admired the Italian frescoes adorning the walls.

"This place is wonderful," she said as she sat down in the seat the hostess had pulled out for her. "It really feels like you are in Italy when you come inside…very charming."

"The owners are from southern Italy —Naples — and they are very proud to have brought many of their family recipes here to the states with them," the hostess explained.

"Fortunate for us," Chloe exclaimed. "There is nothing I love more than authentic Italian food."

Brian beamed in delight that she was so thrilled with the choice of the restaurant. They both ordered a glass of red wine and started to peruse the menus. They decided to split an order of fried calamari to start and then Chloe chose good, old-fashioned chicken parmesan, while Brian decided on the gnocchi, saying it was his absolute favorite.

Dinner went smoothly and both of them commented how amazed they were at how comfortable they felt with each other. They told each other about their families, their lives growing up and even their romances. Chloe shared her experience with Todd and told Brian how strange it had been to see him out last night. She realized she was glad that they had not ended up together. Brian briefly told Chloe about his last serious relationship, a woman he had dated in Law School.

Chloe loved this part of dating — finding out all about someone. She was interested in sharing life stories.

When dessert was finished, they decided to go for a walk at the pier. Brian mentioned that it was his favorite spot, and Chloe agreed that it would be a great place for an after-dinner walk.

"I'll meet you at the pier," he called out to her as they both headed for their cars.

"Sounds good," she responded. "I'll park as close as possible. There shouldn't be many people there now that sunset is over."

Brian waved and nodded in agreement. He was anxious to have a few moments alone in his car to think. He hadn't exactly lied to Chloe at dinner, but he hadn't told her the whole truth, either. He wanted to start out on the right foot with her, but he felt like he had already blown it. He just didn't want to scare her away with the "skeleton in his closet." He knew he had to tell her though, and he figured sooner was probably much better than later.

Once Chloe pulled into a parking spot near the entrance to the pier, she waited anxiously for Brian to arrive. It was such a great date so far, and she was hopeful it would continue along the same path here. Just a moment later, Brian pulled up, and she jumped out of her car to greet him.

"You're a fast driver, huh?" He asked with a cute grin lighting up his face.

"It's the New Yorker in me. I just can't help it. I have been in Florida for a long time now, but I still can't let go of the mentality that everything needs to be done in a rush. It's just part of me."

"Being from the Northeast myself, I'll forgive you." Brian smiled at Chloe as he joked with her and gently put his arm around her back. She smiled back, quite at ease with his intimate gesture.

“This is one of my favorite places to relax and walk on the beach early in the morning. I bring Gabe over before anyone else arrives, and it’s so peaceful. You can often see dolphins feeding at that early time of the morning. It’s Heaven on Earth. I can’t imagine living anywhere else for the rest of my life.”

“You really love it here, huh? I feel the same way. I couldn’t even imagine going back to Connecticut, or any other state, for that matter. I feel like I am truly a Floridian. My family wishes I would head north again, but I can’t do it just for them. I am happy here, but I get back home as much as possible. Do you return to New York a great deal?”

“I try and make it home a few times a year. I like to check out the art exhibitions at the museums, catch a couple of Broadway shows and see my family and friends. Of course, I avoid going at all cost during the really cold months. I just can’t hack the freezing temperatures anymore. Living down here for so long, I have been spoiled.”

“I agree, though I usually make it home for Christmas, regardless of the weather. I don’t think my Mom could handle it if all her children weren’t home for Christmas Day.”

“I guess when you are single, your family expects you to travel to them. Maybe if you were married with a family, it would be different,” she offered.

“Maybe. But my Mom is pretty sentimental about the holidays. She likes everyone to be together no matter what their individual situations. And speaking of being married…Chloe, I have something I need to tell you.”

“Well, ok...for the record, I am glad you didn’t say that you had something to ask me. A marriage proposal on the first date would have been something new for me,” she said then laughed and turned to look at him, noticing he seemed very nervous.

"What is it?" She asked. "You look like you are going to be sick. What are you going to tell me…that you have been married before or something crazy like that?"

As soon as she saw the expression on Brian's face, she regretted her choice of words.

"Actually, that is exactly what I needed to tell you. When we were talking at dinner, I was not exactly honest with you. I mentioned that my last serious relationship was with a woman from Law School, but what I conveniently forgot to mention was that we were married. And after such a colossal failure in choosing the right partner, I'm not sure I'll ever be ready to give it a try again."

"I guess I would call that serious," Chloe said, trying to sound lighthearted to buy herself time to process his confession. Her head was spinning. She knew he was too good to be true, that there had to be a catch somewhere.

And here it was, a problem for her, to be quite honest. Hearing that he had been married didn't fall in line with her idea of a fairytale love story, though she had long ago learned that life didn't always work out as a "happily ever after."

She knew the thing to fear most in a new relationship was the baggage. How much he was carrying from the breakup of his marriage and how deeply he felt betrayed by his ex-wife were the real concerns. Some wounds never heal, and that fact alone didn't bode well for the possibility of them having a meaningful future together.

"I'm surprised. So how long were you married?" She asked, trying to ease the knots in her stomach by learning the facts of the situation.

"It didn't last long, at all. We were divorced in less than a year, and that was five years ago. We made a mistake, and we both realized it quickly. She wanted me to work for a big law firm in New York City, and I wanted to stick to my goal of working in law enforcement. I was very clear about this with her when we met, but I guess she thought I would change my mind. She couldn't understand how anyone with a law degree could choose public service. I should have known it wouldn't work, but I was young, and I felt a lot of pressure from my family. My parents really wanted me to have the joy of a happy marriage and family, like them, and so I gave it a try. I realized a lot of important things during that year, though, and I vowed never to rush into such an important decision, ever again. I'm sorry I didn't tell you about this when we were at dinner, but I didn't want to scare you away. I decided in the car on the way over, however, that it would be better for me to get it out in the open so that you could decide if you want to see me again. I'll understand if you don't want to get involved with someone who has been married already and who struggles with some serious trust issues. I admit that I would have a hard time if you told me that sort of news. By the way, is there anything you need to tell me?" He joked, obviously trying to lighten up the moment.

"Not at all," Chloe replied, maybe too quickly. She certainly didn't want to hurt him. "I don't believe in divorce, per say, especially if children are involved. Though, unfortunately, that wasn't the case for my own parents. They split when I was a teenager, and it broke my heart. My Dad told me the news when I was leaving on a class trip to study at Dolphin Connection for a week one spring break. The beauty of the dolphins kept my heart from totally combusting, along with comforting words from my sister. I also worked with the dolphins to solve a crime during that break, but that is a story for another time. I guess that is why this place has always been so special to me. The first week I ever stayed here, my parents were still together, and I learned that I could be a brave, intelligent person on my own. When I returned home, they speedily finalized their divorce, and my life changed forever. For me, Florida is where my heart is at peace. Hearing that you have been divorced is what it is, and considering the situation, it's understandable. But knowing it has caused you to struggle with trust is a problem. That is hard news to swallow. Do you mind if I take a little while to digest the information? You caught me off guard, and I'm not really sure how I feel about it. Trust ranks high with me. I'd never want to be judged or held accountable for the actions of another woman who wronged you. For my part, I have to be open to the idea that there are men who are trustworthy, despite the despicable behavior I witnessed last night from someone I used to trust. Let's take some time to get to know one another before we make any rash decisions, okay? Why don't we just enjoy the rest of the evening and spend some more time together? Let's assume for now that neither of us are damaged goods beyond repair!"

"Sounds great to me! And thanks for being so understanding, Chloe. Trust is key. At some point, it seems that we will both have to take a leap of faith and learn to trust again. I'm starting to see that it could be worth the risk for the right person. And by the way, what was that you mentioned about solving a crime when you were just a teenager? I didn't know you had a little detective blood running through your veins."

"That is a story for another time. Especially being that it isn't the only crime I've helped solve. You could say that trouble seems to follow me, and I seem to have a knack for figuring out what's happened. I sort of consider it my hobby."

"You consider what I do for a living to be hobby? Thanks a lot!" He joked.

"I didn't mean it like that, at all. I'm sorry. It's just that I like to try and figure things out when something bad happens around me. I like to make sure that the bad guys are brought to justice. And I seem to be pretty good at it."

"I commend your dedication to justice. I'm with you on that note, and I can't wait to hear the stories of your past cases."

"We'll have to wait for a rainy day or two. There are a few stories to tell."

"I can't wait! And by the way, does this mean I should look forward to you poking your nose into the current case at Dolphin Connection?"

"It would be hard for me to stay out of it being that I was the one who found the body!"

"You've got a point there!"

Chloe was amazed to see how relieved Brian was to hear her compassionate words and her diversion into her Nancy Drew Days. A smile came back to his face, and they chatted comfortably as they walked the rest of the way to the end of the pier.

She informed him that she had the next day off and planned to spend it running with Gabe in the morning on the beach and catching up on chores at home. As long as she wasn't called in for any dolphin strandings or manatee rescues, that was her plan. She always put her name on the list of specially-trained volunteers who could help local marine mammals in need.

She hoped her desire to go the extra mile with everything she loved made an impression on him. She knew in her heart that she was someone he could trust, and hoped that he proved to be trustworthy as well. She had already begun to pray on the situation, knowing with conviction that God would lead her in the right direction and send her the answers her heart needed, as always and without fail.

Chapter 15

Chloe woke up earlier than usual for a day off and set out to take Gabe for a run at the beach. She had a lot to accomplish in a short amount of time, and she made a mental list of all she had to do in order to get organized.

She missed having two days off in a row like most working people, but she did enjoy having her choice of days off — a privilege of being one of the senior trainers at Dolphin Connection.

On her first day off of each week, she tried to accomplish her chores: going to the grocery store, cleaning the house and doing the laundry. That way, she could do something enjoyable on her second day off, perhaps working on one of her paintings.

Chloe called to Gabe, grabbed his leash and her iPod and together they headed for the car. He was so excited, he didn't know what to do with himself during the car ride to Siesta Dunes Beach, just a couple of miles from their place. They reached the beach in no time, and she parked her car away from the other beach goers. She tried very hard to keep the Mustang in good condition and didn't want it to get dinged by other car doors.

"We're here Gabe," she announced. She got out of the car as Gabe scurried to jump out at the same time. It was a ritual for him. He was so happy to reach the beach, he would basically spill out of the car.

"Go for it!" Chloe called to him as he started to run towards the water. "There is no one else here right now, boy, so take advantage of it. You know the drill. If one person or dog comes, you go on your leash."

Gabe nodded his head, appearing as if he understood what she said. That or his head bobbed at just the right time. Either way, he took off at maximum speed and ran into the surf.

It wasn't common for poodles to like the ocean, but Gabe couldn't get enough of it. Ever since they moved to Florida years earlier, he'd enjoyed the water. Maybe because the water was so warm and inviting. He hadn't really taken to the frigid waters up in Maine where they used to vacation before they moved to the South.

Chloe enjoyed watching him as he paddled into the waves. He knew just the right moment to duck under the rising white water before a wave crashed upon him. She often wished that the dolphins she would see swimming in pods and fishing early in the morning might pop up and give him a visit. Of course, she wasn't quite sure what he would do if that happened. It might scare him half to death.

He had been introduced to the marine mammal residents of Dolphin Connection, and he wasn't quite sure what to make of them. Tango & Cash had zoomed by the dock to splash him and then quickly returned for their fish reward. Gabe didn't know whether to be upset that they had gotten him wet or try to steal their lunch. He was quite confused. Chloe laughed all to herself as she remembered the experience.

Before she could get too lost in her thoughts, though, Gabe was running out of the water waiting for her to throw his ball, bringing her back to the moment. They walked great distances this way with him running out of the water and her throwing his ball a little bit further down the beach into the surf.

Chloe had a lot on her mind. She wasn't sure how to feel about the situation with Brian. She knew things seemed too good to be true. He was a good looking, smart and interesting single man. Of course, there had to be a stumbling block.

God seemed to offer them to make her slow down and really think things through in her life. Being human, she wasn't always thrilled by the challenge. Though she knew, through her faith, every challenge had a purpose.

She didn't know why it bothered her so much that he had been previously married. He had made a mistake. Everybody makes mistakes. She knew he hadn't done anything wrong, but she had always hoped or maybe even just assumed that the man of her dreams, the man she would marry (if Brian was that man) would never have been married, either. She knew it didn't really matter, but she also knew it was okay to give herself time to process the news. Her main concern still pushed at her thoughts. She didn't want to fall in love with him, only to find out he couldn't let himself trust a woman again or take another chance at marriage.

The morning flew by as she and Gabe soaked in their time on the beach together. Gabe was reluctant to get in the car to leave, but Chloe knew he was tired and ready to get home for a big drink and a long nap on his favorite blanket. She would listen to him snore contentedly and use the time to clean her apartment.

After hydrating himself with a large bowl of spring water as soon as they arrived home, he did as she expected and retired to his beloved bed — a luxurious, down comforter with his name embroidered on it.

Chloe moved quickly through her apartment, trying to get her cleaning done in record time. She was always amazed at the amount of tidying up there was to do for just her and Gabe. Usually, she found the process of cleaning relaxing and somewhat gratifying because a job well done could be visibly recognized, but today she simply wanted to complete her chores so that she could get to her studies.

She planned on spending most of the afternoon pouring over the notes for the Research Seminar. She had decided to bring them home to give them closer attention than she had time to at work. For some reason, something was bothering her about the content of the class she presented the previous day, but she just couldn't put her finger on it. She wondered whether it had any connection at all to Molly's case, and she knew she wouldn't rest well until she figured it out.

She read and reread the notes, but nothing specific jumped off the pages at her. Nonetheless, something continued to tug at her gut. She felt like she was missing the piece of the puzzle that was the solution to the case.

Out of the corner of her eye, she spotted the clock and gasped when she realized it was much later than she thought. Brian had called during the day, and they had made plans to meet for drinks that night at a local bar. She still had to walk and feed Gabe and get herself pulled together. She'd have to put the class notes away for now and return to them later.

"Let's go Gabe," she called as she grabbed his leash and a baggie and headed towards the front door. Gabe jumped up from his afternoon nap and stretched out before meeting her at the front door.

"How are you doing, buddy?" She asked him as she knelt to pat him and hook his leash to his collar. He wriggled around and wagged his tail, letting her know he was just fine. They headed out the door together to enjoy their afternoon walk. It would have to be a quick one, though. She didn't have much time before she was to meet

Brian at Burdine’s, a great local hangout, just a few minutes from her place.

Chapter 16

Brian was waiting for Chloe at the front door of Burdine's when she arrived just a wee bit fashionably late.

"Hi there," she piped-up as she walked up to meet him, giving him a casual kiss on the cheek.

"Hi, glad you made it," he said. "I was beginning to worry that you weren't coming after the news I dumped on you last night."

"The news was a little surprising at first, but I've had some time to decide that I'm okay with it. You're a great guy, and you deserve a shot at a successful relationship. Quite frankly, we both do. Besides, I'm not the type of girl who just doesn't show up for a date. I would have called to let you know if I wasn't coming."

"I know," he said. "But I was worried, none the less. I'm just glad I didn't blow it between us by bringing up my past. I wanted to be up front and honest with you."

"I am a firm believer that honesty truly is the best policy. It is always better to know the whole truth about someone than be in the dark. But enough of this heavy talk. Let's allow trust to build between us organically and see if each of us can leave our past behind. I'm here to watch a beautiful sunset with you and to share some good drinks and great seafood."

"You're right! Let's see if we can get a table outside by the water. It is a perfect night to relax out on the deck. After you," he said as he held the door open for her.

They walked through the restaurant and found the hostess for the outdoor section. Chloe was amazed by the number of indoor diners, considering it was such a beautiful night. She could never understand how some Floridians simply became tired of the sunny, warm weather and preferred the comfort of air conditioning over the great outdoors. She spent every drop of time she could soaking up the Florida sunshine.

"Here we go," directed the hostess as she showed them to a table with an excellent view of the horizon…perfect for sunset.

Brian turned and thanked the hostess before pulling out Chloe's chair for her.

"What an old-fashioned gentleman you are," Chloe teased. "It is hard to find a man who still treats a lady the right way. Your Dad must have taught you well."

"He really did in every way possible. He and my Mom are still in love to this day, after 40 years of marriage. My Dad always goes out of his way to make my Mom feel special, and she does the same for him. There's a mutual respect there that I couldn't identify as a child, but I could definitely feel it. They really enjoy each other's company, which is quite rare today."

"Then I'll have to thank them for raising such a kind gentleman. I appreciate the little things a great deal, and you seem to be the type of person who goes out of his way to take care of the little things. I like to do the same for the people I care about."

The waitress came over as Chloe was finishing her sentence which was sort of a relief because she was almost embarrassed by the seriousness of their conversation, once again. She didn't want Brian to think she was being too sappy at the beginning of their relationship; though she was truly touched by his thoughtfulness.

The waitress introduced herself as Emily and took their drink orders. She quickly returned with their beer and the conch fritter appetizers they'd ordered as well. They toasted to the impending sunset and munched on their fritters as the sun dipped lower in the sky. As they drank their beer and relaxed into a casual conversation, the sun finally dropped out of sight in the distance.

Everyone cheered as they do for every sunset in Florida and Brian smiled at Chloe with an amused expression on his face. "I think I just saw the green flash," he said to her in a rather surprised tone.

"That's what that was! Yes! I saw it, too! Wow! That's awesome! You need just the right conditions to see the flash. It is very rare and said to be good luck. I say we toast the green flash and the good luck it will bring to us."

They clinked their glasses together and showed each other very happy smiles.

"Everybody needs good luck. We couldn't have planned to see the flash if we had tried. It just has to happen, and it did for us. I like that," Chloe said, knowing it was a sign from above that they'd shared this rare experience.

"Me, too. So, tell me what you did on your day off. Did you get a lot accomplished?" Brian asked.

"I did knock a lot of things off my list," she explained, "but there never seems to be enough time to get everything done. Gabe and I spent a long time at the beach this morning and then I got my housecleaning out of the way. This afternoon, I worked on the notes for a class we teach to our students that come to train at Dolphin Connection. Molly used to teach the seminar, and they asked me to take it over this week because it was on the students' schedule for the day after she died. Something is bugging me about the seminar, though, and I just can't figure it out. How is the case going? Are there any leads?"

“Not much new information has come to the forefront, but we still have a lot of ground to cover. Why do you think there is something fishy about the seminar notes?”

“I can’t put my finger on it just yet, but there is something that doesn’t seem right. Molly hadn’t been at Dolphin Connection very long when she died, but from her notes on the seminar, there was definitely something bothering her. I’m just not sure what it was or what she was trying to do about it. She wasn’t very outgoing at work, as I mentioned when you first interviewed me, and so I really don’t know what was going on in her life. She didn’t go out with the other staff members when we all got together to hang out or celebrate a special occasion. She basically kept to herself and concentrated on her job. She seemed to like what she was doing and took her job quite seriously. She was a real ‘straight and narrow’ kind of person, very focused on her own little corner of the world. She absolutely loved the dolphins, though. Sometimes, she would come in on her days off just to spend more time with them. A great deal of her job kept her behind the scenes, and she really seemed to cherish the time she spent interacting with all the beautiful grey faces at our facility. I tried to go out of my way to give her as much interaction as possible with feeding sessions and signals practice. Since she wasn’t part of the training department, she needed a trainer with her to do more hands-on sessions with the dolphins. She always seemed to appreciate the extra time I made possible for her to spend with the dolphins. Of course, anyone who loves dolphins has a special place in my heart.”

“How about someone who didn’t even know he loved dolphins before, but now realizes how much he has been missing?” Brian asked with his sweet grin in place, melting Chloe’s heart even more.

"Oh, I think I could make just as much room in my heart for a convert. After all, it's not your fault that you never had the opportunity to get to know some of God's most wonderful creatures before you met me. I'll just take it as another positive reason that our lives came together."

"I agree," Brian said and nodded. "I really feel like this is the beginning of something special. The incident that brought us together was most unfortunate, but it seems to have happened for a reason. I think your insight to and knowledge of Dolphin Connection is really going to help me solve this case. I usually operate quite independently when I investigate a crime, but I never turn down valuable information. Your description of Molly's personality and work habits are very helpful. A good detective really needs to understand the ins and outs of a victim's life in order to figure out his or her death. Molly doesn't sound like the type of person who would have knowingly gotten herself into trouble or made enemies. If her death wasn't a random act of violence, which is still a distinct possibility, then she must have upset somebody very deeply without being aware she'd done so."

"It is strange that such a quiet, sensible person could be involved in such a violent crime. I can't imagine who would have had a reason to specifically cause this type of harm to a person like her. It makes much more sense that it was a random act of violence, but what doesn't make sense is how a stranger could have gotten on the grounds of Dolphin Connection after hours. That would be a pretty hard thing to do, considering that our closedown procedure at night is very strict. The manager of the gift shop and ticket sales checks every last inch of the grounds each evening at 5 PM, just to make sure that doesn't happen. We had an incident occur about two years ago when several local teenagers decided to hide in the bathroom one evening so that they wouldn't have to leave the grounds. When the last staff member left, the kids had their own dolphin swims and caused such a raucous, they alarmed the neighbors whose homes border the facility. Evidently, the dolphins were screeching quite loudly because they were so annoyed by them. The evenings are supposed to be the time of day when the dolphins have the place to themselves, and they didn't appreciate having that time interrupted by a bunch of rowdy teenagers who rudely invaded their space and didn't even bring any fish along as a peace offering. Luckily, the Police arrived in time to catch them in the act, and they were arrested for trespassing and animal endangerment. Fortunately, none of the dolphins were injured, but everyone on the staff was so upset by the incident that Shannon and Theresa put our present closing procedures into place and installed cameras in key locations to monitor all activity in the dolphin lagoons. Anyone who lives in the area knows what happened and knows what has been done to make sure it never happens again. We haven't had a problem since."

"Certainly, it would have been quite difficult for a stranger to have gotten on the grounds and been the one to kill Molly, though not impossible. But it seems even stranger that one of the staff at Dolphin Connection is responsible. We have interviewed every single person, and I just can't seem to find anything suspicious. People who dedicate their lives to help animals and make little pay for it aren't your typical criminals. And being that the cameras you mentioned were only there to protect the dolphins by filming the lagoons, they have been of no use in our investigation."

"I couldn't agree with you more about our staff. I am very close with them, and there isn't one person I could even imagine doing something so horrific. The whole thing just doesn't make sense to me. Even worse, I can't seem to shake this uneasiness deep in my stomach that has lingered since first seeing Molly's lifeless body."

"Crimes never make sense, even when you do figure them out. Especially, when the perpetrator is someone you would never suspect. Someone who committed the crime in the heat of passion or simply didn't think the situation through before taking action. The one thing that is consistent is that the perpetrator always has a reason, an explanation for why they thought they had to commit the crime. The sad thing is when they start to explain it, it becomes apparent even to them that there is never reason enough to take another person's life."

"That is sad, but very true, I imagine. Your work must be interesting in many ways, but depressing in others. You see people at their worst, but you put the clues together to solve the crime and bring the victims and their families justice."

"I couldn't have said it better myself," Brian said, taking a deep breath as if totally satisfied with their conversation.

They had been so engrossed in their conversation that they didn't even see the waitress standing at their table trying to get a word in edgewise.

"May I take those plates for you?" She asked.

"Sure," they said together as they moved out of the way so that she could pick up the remnants of their appetizers. Somehow, in the midst of all their talking, they had managed to eat every bite of food in front of them.

"May I get you anything else?" The waitress asked as she picked up their plates.

Brian looked Chloe's way to see if she was interested in the offer, but she shook her head no. "I'm full. How about you?"

"I'm all set as well, may we just take the check when you get a chance please, Emily?"

"I'll have it right out to you. Have a great evening now."

"Would you like to get something for dessert?" Brian asked. "I have a real sweet tooth, I'm sorry to say."

"Oh, don't be sorry. I have an unbelievable sweet tooth, too. Have you tried the new ice cream café Sprinkles? You can make your own sundae."

"I haven't gotten there yet, but I have been meaning to stop by."

"Oh, then you are just a lightweight when it comes to sweets. I'm already their best customer," Chloe said.

Brian laughed as he finished paying the bill and then they both got up from the table.

"Why don't you follow me to Sprinkles and then we can decide where we want to go from there?" Chloe suggested.

"Sounds like a plan," he said as he smiled and escorted her out of Burdine's. "And maybe next time, you'll let me pick you up at your apartment like a proper date. I've been eager to meet Gabe."

"That seems reasonable," Chloe said, not wanting to rush into anything.

Driving her own car when they went out helped her feel more secure and independent. She was confident she could now let Brian into her life, but Gabe would be the one to put him to the real test.

Chapter 17

Chloe's alarm clock sent her flying out of bed the next morning.

Usually, she woke up long before it went off, only setting it for backup. She had enjoyed her evening with Brian so much that she had stayed out much later than she liked to on a work night.

After they both gobbled their sundaes at Sprinkles, they returned to the pier for an evening stroll. This time, they spent a lot more time kissing and a lot less time talking about the past or the case they were both trying to solve.

Chloe immediately called to Gabe as she jumped out of bed. He was sleeping on his own bed and comforter that were right next to her bed. He stretched as he stood up, shook himself out and was as fresh as ever.

She was always amazed at how easily he could wake up. "Come on, buddy. Mommy is going to have to really get moving if she is going to make it to work on time."

Gabe seemed to understand just what she said and headed straight for the front door for his walk. As soon as she had changed into her tank top and shorts — her usual work uniform, Chloe followed behind him. They took their usual path, and Gabe took care of his business. She quickly fed him his breakfast, grabbed a bite herself and flew out the front door with her work bag. She was already in the car when she realized that she had forgotten to brush her teeth. She quickly ran back upstairs. Gabe was delighted to see her, but he thought she was home for good.

"Sorry, buddy," she called as she went flying by him on her way to the bathroom. "I just forgot to brush my teeth, and I couldn't go through the whole day with them gritty."

Gabe sighed as if he had accepted that his best friend wouldn't be staying home, after all. He was probably just glad he wasn't the one who needed to get his teeth brushed, one of his least favorite activities after going to the vet and the poodle parlor.

Chloe called goodbye to him on her way out the door, but he barely lifted his head in acknowledgement. She skipped down her front steps, jumped into her car and made it to work in record time.

She was on the "Catch Team" that morning and had about ten minutes to drop off her bag, slip on a wet suit and make it down to the dock of the assigned dolphins. The dolphins who had to be "caught" or placed in a stretcher with the help of the trainers and other staff members were those who had gastrointestinal issues and weren't eating enough on their own.

Chloe checked the schedule and saw that it was Rainbow, one of their older males who was to be caught. He often gave the trainers a tough time, so she readied herself for the encounter. Either Shannon or Theresa orchestrated all of the catches. Today, it was Shannon, which Chloe was glad to see, since she was usually a bit more laid back at these sessions than her sister.

Shannon was firm with the dolphin in need, but also understanding when things didn't go perfectly the first time. Theresa usually lost her cool and so the staff preferred when Shannon was in charge in hopes they wouldn't get their heads chopped off. Since Shannon was married with children, she didn't seem to be quite as uptight about the operation of the facility as Theresa.

Shannon loved the dolphins, but she had a lot of distractions.

Shannon started assigning roles and Chloe took her position holding the head of the stretcher. Other staff members held long nets which, on Shannon's command, were gently used to coerce Rainbow into a smaller and smaller area. Once Rainbow was brought into a confined area of the shallow section of the lagoon, he was given a moment to calm down before two of the larger, male staff members took a firm hold of him and transferred him to the stretcher.

The whole process went smoothly, and Rainbow didn't even thrash as he was brought over and placed into the stretcher. Once he was in place, Shannon handed Chloe a tube, which she inserted into Rainbow's rostrum (mouth) and down his esophagus. Since dolphins do not have a gag reflex, this was much easier than it would be with a human patient. Chloe had done the procedure many times over the years and was skilled at getting the tube down past the goose beak, the physiological part of a dolphin that separates their trachea from their esophagus. That is probably why Shannon and Theresa always chose her for this position.

Sometimes, Chloe tried to teach other trainers how to insert the tube, but many of them were understandably uncomfortable with the procedure. They preferred that she keep this role, and so did the dolphins it seemed. They didn't like when inexperienced trainers attempted to tube them. It just added another layer of stress to the process of being caught by humans and being placed in a stretcher.

Rainbow was in a cooperative mood and took his liquids and medicine quickly and easily. He was quite relieved, though, when Shannon told all of the staff members on the stretcher to lower it into the water and let him go. He immediately swam off in his graceful fashion and headed clear to the other side of the lagoon. He seemed to want to get as far away from his human friends as possible. This, of course, was normal behavior after such a procedure.

Dolphins like to reassert their independence following a controlled interaction with humans. Fortunately, for many of them, the procedure with the stretcher was no longer required. They were trained to voluntarily come to the dock to receive any necessary fluids.

"Hey, everybody," Shannon called out, "great job today. Thanks for making Rainbow's catch progress so smoothly. We'll monitor his fish intake in the next few days and see how he does eating on his own. Hopefully, his meds will calm down his stomach ulcer. But, as we all know, if he doesn't eat enough on his own, we'll have to catch him again. We don't want him to become dehydrated, and no fish means no water intake. Keep your fingers crossed for the increased health of our beautiful boy."

People started walking away as Shannon finished speaking. Most of the staff had to get changed and get to the business of their usual days.

"Hold on, everyone," Shannon spoke up. "I also wanted to mention that we will have an emergency staff meeting today at 5 PM. We apologize for the last-minute notice, but it is imperative that each and every staff member attend. The meeting will be held in the lounge area of the trainer's office. If anyone has a conflict at that time, please speak with either Theresa or myself to see if we can work something out. I look forward to seeing all of you this evening. Have a great day!"

Everyone moved out because it was getting late, and the facility was opening to the public soon. Chloe followed the others, grabbed her bag and went to change into a dry bathing suit. She had a long day ahead of her and always felt better when she made a fresh start.

The day flew by, and Chloe had fun as always interacting with the dolphins through training and feeding sessions. Her favorite part of the day of course was play time, but even then, her mind was never far from the meeting that Shannon had announced for that afternoon.

As she tossed a pink hula hoop and purple scarf to Persy and watched the delicate dolphin "dress up," her thoughts continued to wander. Only when Rainbow came over and gave her a big tail splash did she really come back to the moment. A tail splash from a 9-foot dolphin wasn't something to be ignored!

Rainbow wanted Chloe to toss her his favorite football, and she did so immediately. She was relieved to see him active and alert for that meant the fluids they had given him earlier had been effective. She tossed him the football and then played frisbee with him. There were no shortage of toys for the dolphins at the facility. Their fans near and wide kept them plush with gifts from around the world.

Chloe had assumed the meeting that evening was planned to discuss the aftereffects of Molly's death. She thought the meeting should have been held right after the incident occurred, but better late than never, she supposed. She also knew Brian would be very interested in the content of the meeting, and she planned to pay very close attention to what people said. She intended to ask questions of her own that might stir up some discussion.

Chloe needed to find out what other people felt about this horrible thing that had happened to one of their fellow colleagues. They had all been immediately instructed to be quiet the day after the incident, so she hadn't been able to gauge at all how the others felt…how they truly felt. She hoped to get some revealing emotional responses from them later that day.

Chapter 18

"Come on in, Chloe," Shannon called across the room as Chloe entered the trainer's lounge for the meeting. She had intended to be early, but Tango & Cash had become very silly at her last training session and she had spent a lot more time with them than she had planned.

As she grabbed a glass of water and found a comfy seat near her friends, Shannon called the meeting to order.

"I can't believe Theresa isn't taking charge. Sitting back and letting Shannon run the meeting is so out of character…for both of them," Chloe's friend Amy whispered in her ear.

Chloe nodded in agreement, but she didn't say a word. She shot Amy a look to remind her that she didn't like to gossip during work hours, especially in the middle of a meeting called by the Directors themselves.

Amy rolled her eyes as if mildly annoyed at Chloe's goody-two-shoes attitude. Chloe didn't mind if other people made fun of her for her strict work ethic. Her hard work, dedication and kindness had helped her progress successfully in her career at a quick pace, and she didn't want that to change.

As she heard Shannon start to explain why the evening's meeting had been called, she snapped out of her thoughts.

"I would like to thank everybody for adjusting their schedules and being here this evening. We do appreciate your flexibility. This has been a difficult week for all of us. We have been shocked and saddened by Molly's murder and totally outraged that this type of violent crime could take place on the grounds of our facility. Of course, our priority is always the health and well-being of our dolphins, and we needed to keep things as normal as possible following this horrible incident so that each and every one of our beautiful grey faces felt safe and secure. You all mean the world to us, but we all know when we choose to work with marine animals, that like our children, their safety and well-being comes before our own. There were a lot of strange people on the grounds the night of the murder, and it had to be especially disturbing for our animals because it happened during 'dolphin time,' the sacred hours when they have the facility all to themselves."

Shannon continued, seeming anxious to get through with the meeting and onto other things, "We asked all of you to act basically as if nothing had happened so that the dolphins would have consistency and normalcy in their schedules and keep their stress levels down, not because we didn't care about Molly. We in no way want you all to think that we weren't just as upset by Molly's death as all of you. We are thankful that many of you have spoken with Detective White, the local authority who is leading the investigation for this case. I spoke with him earlier today, and he mentioned that everybody has been forthcoming with him and that he hoped to speak with several people again. The Detectives and Crime Scene Investigators worked through the night on the evening of the murder because we needed to be ready to open to the public the next morning and provide the dolphins with a stable environment. If something new develops with the investigation, you may see one of them on the grounds of the facility again. They will make sure they are as unobtrusive as possible. There is not much to share yet, though Detective White does think this was an isolated incident and feels that each of you are perfectly safe here on the grounds of the facility. In the past, we have followed a very strict closing policy, and we are going to be tightening up a few loose ends that still exist. We want to make sure that there is never a solitary staff member on the grounds in the early morning or in the evening."

Chloe was dismayed by this news, as she was often one of the first to arrive in the morning and the last one out in the evening. She loved her private time with the dolphins and was saddened that this time had now vanished in front of her eyes.

Shannon shot her an understanding look as if she knew what she was thinking.

"Hopefully, this won't be a permanent situation, but, for now, it is necessary. Either Theresa or I will be here each morning to open and each evening to close. This will be a major adjustment to each of our schedules as well. If it doesn't work out, we have considered having a plain-clothes security guard on the grounds at all times. We never thought we would have to do something like that here at Dolphin Connection, but the world has changed a lot in recent years, and we have to adapt in order to keep our dolphins and each other safe."

She continued, hardly coming up for air, "We are also going to ask that each staff member checks in or out when he or she leaves the property on a work-related or personal errand. In the past, we have been relaxed about our policies with staff members using breaks to take care of personal needs. Theresa and I feel that it is important to be flexible and supportive, and we understand that many of you have second jobs in order to pay your bills, which makes your schedules very tight. Those second jobs, of course, leave you little time to take care of personal matters that come up. If you can accomplish a task during your break and get to your next assignment on schedule, then we continue to have no problem with this policy. We are simply going to ask you to sign out and in at a register log that will be at the front desk of the gift shop, in addition to notifying your Department Supervisor. This way, Theresa and I have an easy way to check the whereabouts of each staff member in the case of an emergency. The last safety measure we are going to take is to discontinue the use of the employee gate. It has never posed a problem in the past, but we have been advised to have all staff use one common entrance and exit, for the time being. Of course, that will be through the front door of the gift shop, the main entrance and exit to our facility for all of us and our guests. We know that this will be an annoyance to many of you, but it does seem to be necessary at this point. Having an employee gate with a pad lock on it may have been the reason we had an uninvited guest on the grounds who is responsible for Molly's death. We don't think any of you intentionally let in a stranger, but we have had instances in the past where the combination to the lock has mysteriously spread around town and times when the lock was left open for the convenience of the next person in or out. We have discussed this problem in the past and tried to be flexible about it. But we now must insist that all staff use the gift shop entrance until another solution is found. Please allow yourself a few extra minutes in the morning since the main door can get clogged with early guests. Please also make sure that you are packed and ready to go at the end of the day promptly at 5:45 PM. That should give everyone enough time to finish up their last sessions by 5:30 PM, clean up and gather their things to head home. Are there any questions?"

Shannon said these last words more as a courtesy rather than an actual invitation, judging by her rather dismissive tone. Since she was picking up her bag and gesturing for everyone else to do the same, it appeared she was more interested in wrapping up the meeting than hearing questions.

Chloe had been at Dolphin Connection long enough not to be put off by Shannon's flighty ways. Usually, she was more worried about getting home to her husband and children than listening to the gripes of the staff. She was certainly the more relaxed of the two sisters during the day, when the job wasn't interfering with her family duties, but everyone knew it was Theresa who considered Dolphin Connection to be her family, and, for her, it always came first. Theresa could be tough on her staff at times, but she was always fair and loved to reward a job well done.

Theresa noticed Chloe's hand in the air and motioned for everyone to stay seated. She made it quite clear that the meeting was not over, which visibly annoyed her sister.

"Go ahead, Chloe," Theresa encouraged as she smiled in Chloe's direction.

Everyone knew Theresa admired Chloe's strong work ethic and her love for the dolphins. They had never clashed, not once in all her years of employment.

"Thanks, Theresa. This won't take long. I just have a couple of points I want to make."

"There is no rush, Chloe," Theresa interrupted as she shot a firm sideways glance at her restless sister.

"Thanks. First, I am glad that you all decided to hold this meeting tonight and that we are discussing this matter. As some of you may know, I am the one who found Molly's body in the bathroom stall last Wednesday evening. It was a very scary situation, to say the least, when I realized that Molly's killer might still be on the grounds, and I was alone. I agree with the idea that we need some tighter security measures, at least until we find out what happened. That brings me to my second point, which actually is a question. I wanted to ask all staff members to think about something for me. I have taken over the Research Seminar until we have a new person in Molly's old position. I have spent a number of hours over the last week reviewing the materials for the seminar because it has been a while and I needed a little refresher."

On that note, many of the other trainers nodded in agreement, knowing they would have to do the same if they were unexpectedly asked to teach a seminar outside their area of expertise.

"It seems to me, from reading Molly's notes, that something was bugging her here at Dolphin Connection. She was so quiet and to herself that I can't really put my finger on it, but I think she was trying to figure out something. I really can't say why I feel this way, nor do I have any concrete evidence, but it is just a gut feeling and usually my gut feelings are right. If you have any idea of what was possibly troubling her, please let the detectives know. It may be crucial to the investigation of her death."

"Now then…if Chloe is done expressing her gut feelings, maybe we can call it a night!" Shannon said in an obviously annoyed tone that caught everyone off guard.

Chloe was shocked by Shannon's outburst and rather hurt. It was so out of character for her. She didn't know if she had crossed some line by bringing up this last point without running it by Shannon or Theresa first or maybe Shannon was just really ticked off that it was getting later and later, and she wasn't home to her family yet. Either way, her little quip was unprofessional and seemed to put everyone in the room in the middle of an awkward silence.

"Sounds like somebody is getting a little grouchy around dinner time." Theresa broke the mood, trying to make up for her sister's inappropriate remark. "Why don't you grab one of the snacks we put out so that your blood sugar level doesn't drop any lower, Shannon?"

Theresa shot Shannon a look that could kill, and Shannon begrudgingly went over to the wonderful array of snacks that had been set out. She looked like a dog that had been scolded, walking away with her tail between her legs.

"You were saying, Chloe," Theresa nodded at her thoughtfully to continue.

Chloe was so caught off guard by Shannon's outburst that she lost her train of thought. She had to collect herself before she could continue.

"Um, uh, I was pretty much done, I think." She paused for a moment and then her last point came back to her. "As mentioned in your official memo the other day, I am hoping to do something special in Molly's memory. I know that she was only here a short time, but she was a dedicated staff member during her tenure and she seemed to be a very decent human being. It would be nice to have some sort of memorial in her honor, if we could pull together the money to make it possible. If everyone could donate maybe $20 and contribute ideas, I would be more than happy to coordinate the effort and make sure a memorial takes place."

"Thank you for taking charge of that, Chloe. Is there anyone who would like to make a different suggestion or is everyone okay with the idea of a memorial?" Theresa asked.

All the trainers and the other department members nodded in agreement that a memorial was a good thing to do for Molly.

"Thanks again for offering to take care of everything, Chloe. You are right that it is important to do something here for us to remember Molly. I'm sorry I didn't have more time to get to know her myself, but as you said, she was a kind person with a huge heart for the dolphins. She was always ready to go above and beyond her duties for the sake of those wonderful animals out there," Bailey shared as she smiled at Chloe and nodded towards the dolphin lagoons.

"Thanks, Bailey, for your encouragement," Chloe responded, "and my gratitude to everyone in advance for your participation in the memorial project."

The rest of the group nodded and smiled in Chloe's direction. She felt the warmth and support of her colleagues — one of the reasons, next to her love for the dolphins, that she enjoyed her time at Dolphin Connection so much.

"Are there any other thoughts or concerns?" Theresa asked the crowd.

By this time, Shannon looked like she was ready to burst. It was getting to be well-past dinner time, and she couldn't stop checking her watch. Chloe thought to herself that she must be missing something pretty important to make such a spectacle of herself. This type of behavior was not only inappropriate, but so out of character for her. Chloe just couldn't figure it out.

The voice of one of her friends from the Education Department, Eliza, brought her out of her thoughts.

"I did some work with Molly when she first came on board to make sure she was fully prepared to teach the class. I was happy to spend the extra time with her since I had worked in research before I transferred over to education. Molly was very ambitious about revamping the whole seminar. It was her main focus here, and she had the expertise because of the graduate degree she received. She mentioned that she was going to start at the beginning and make the seminar more interesting and more interactive for students. I don't know how far she had gotten with the revisions because I didn't have much interaction with her after that time. Maybe you and I could get together, Chloe, and go over the notes you have from her. I could probably make some distinctions for you between what was part of the old seminar and what she had developed."

Chloe thanked her friend for the information and suggested that they get together as soon as possible to review the notes, knowing time was of the essence in a murder investigation. Chloe knew there was more information to be gleaned from the research material, and she hoped a fresh set of eyes would be the key. Brian would be thankful, too, for any pertinent observations.

Theresa thanked Eliza for her input as well and then made sure there weren't any other staff members who wanted to talk. When it was clear that nobody else had any further comments to make, she thanked everyone for their attendance and brought the meeting to an end. She invited everyone to stay for a bit longer and socialize and enjoy the food and drinks they had provided.

The staff looked happy to be able to get up from their seats and move towards the food. Chloe's colleagues had the munchies on a continuous basis, as did she. She found herself pouring a large cup of fruit punch and eyeing an array of goodies when she noticed Theresa and Shannon having a heated conversation by the door. Theresa seemed to be scolding Shannon like a child who had stepped out of line. After Shannon's embarrassing behavior, though, Chloe didn't blame Theresa. When she noticed Chloe staring in their direction, their conversation came to an abrupt end. Theresa smiled curtly at her sister and gave her a gentle push out the door. She then moved discreetly towards the rest of the crowd and mingled.

"Earth to Chloe!"

Chloe was startled by her friend's hand on her back.

"Hey, Eliza, what's up?"

"What had your attention? The feuding sisters?"

"Something was really out of whack between the two of them tonight. Their personalities and styles have always been so different, but that is what made their partnership work so well. They balanced each other out and always seemed to accept each other's differences."

"Very true. It must be something outside of work that put Shannon in such a foul mood this evening. Maybe she is having problems at home. Whatever it is, Theresa didn't seem happy that she let her personal issues affect her at work. That was definitely an uncomfortable meeting."

"I know," agreed Chloe. "Maybe I shouldn't have spoken up. But these issues about Molly have been in the forefront of my mind for the last week, and it seemed urgent that I express them while all of us were present."

"You did the right thing, Chloe. I was surprised they waited almost a week to hold the meeting. It seemed to me it should have been held immediately after the incident."

"I agree. And I can't quite figure that one out for myself. It is a touchy situation at a facility like this one when something like this occurs. The welfare of the dolphins and the enjoyment of the guests have to come first, and I suppose that makes things different than they might be at an organization that doesn't focus on animals. Though, I still don't like how it was handled, I'm sure they did their best."

"Very true. You always have a way of seeing the positive or the sensible in things Chloe."

"Only after lots of thought and consideration. It doesn't just come to me. But once I remember that there is a reason and an explanation for everything that happens on this Earth, then things make much more sense."

"You really think that's true, don't you?' Eliza asked. "You always seem to find a rhyme and a reason for everything that happens in your life."

"It is the only way I know to bring order to this chaotic mess we call life. It helps me see that there's a purpose in everything. It's so strange, but even Molly's tragic death has caused something significant to happen in my life."

"What do you mean, Chloe? You have my curiosity aroused."

"Well, I guess it's okay to talk about it at this point. I'm dating the lead detective on Molly's investigation. We met the night of the murder because I stayed on the grounds until Theresa, and later Shannon, arrived. Brian, that's his name, was very understanding regarding my shock over witnessing the crime scene, and he spent time questioning me on the docks. He stayed with me until I calmed down. We had this incredible, immediate attraction to one another. He smiled at me in the midst of this horrible situation, and I saw my future laid out in front of me. It was the strangest thing I have ever experienced. It really has startled me."

"Did he ask you out that night?"

"No, not at all. Once the sisters arrived, he focused his attention on speaking with them and monitoring the Crime Scene Investigators. I was told that I could go home and did so quietly. I didn't know if I'd ever see him again, but for some reason that didn't bother me. Our encounter had been magical and stirred feelings inside me that I thought had been put to rest when I left New York."

"You are much too young to think you would never fall in love again. That jerk from college caused your heart more damage than I had previously realized. But, moving on... how did you and Brian end up crossing paths?"

"Bailey and I met for dinner and drinks the next evening at The Hurricane, the evening you weren't able to make it, and I literally bumped into him on the way out. We had a drink together and talked like we had known each other for years. We have seen each other every night since."

"Wow! That is unbelievable. What are the odds?"

"No odds, Eliza. We were supposed to meet. I can't help but think our lives came together for a reason. The strange thing is that I also ran into 'the jerk from college' that same day. Now a married family man, he was in the area on business and ended up on my tour that afternoon. Just the sight of him overwhelmed me with emotions. We caught up and seemingly the door to that part of my life was closed for good. Imagine my surprise that evening when I caught a glimpse of him at The Hurricane flirting with a young colleague. I was so relieved we hadn't ended up together. When I ran into Brian on my way out of the restaurant, my life came full circle."

"Well, you have me convinced, once and for all. Everything does happen for a reason. So, when do I get to meet this wonderful man of your dreams?"

"Let's not jump to conclusions. Though that's certainly my hope!" Chloe confided in her friend.

"You're smitten, Chloe. I should have recognized it earlier. I know that look, and I'm so happy for you. This has been a long time coming, and you deserve it more than anyone I know."

"Thanks, Eliza. You're a great friend. I would love for you to meet Brian, and I think he would be eager to hear any input you have about the Research Seminar. Let's get together for lunch tomorrow to go over things first and then maybe we can meet up with him in the evening."

"Great! Why don't you guys come over to my place, and I'll order some pizzas and sodas."

"Perfect. I'll check with him and call you at home later to confirm."

"Sounds good. Let's grab some more munchies before we duck out of here."

"I'm right behind you. Hey, Eliza, how come you didn't meet Brian during the interview sessions?"

"He and his partner split up the staff members to make the process move more quickly. I heard his name mentioned, but I never met him because he was conducting interviews in another room."

"That makes sense. Well then, you'll be in for a treat when you meet him tomorrow night!"

Chapter 19

Chloe was more than relieved when she arrived home and walked through her front door. Home sweet home made ever sweeter by the incredible reception she received from her favorite little guy in the world.

"Hey, Gabe. How are you, buddy? Mommy's sorry she's late. Did Ann come and see you this afternoon? When I found out I had a meeting this evening, I called her, and she promised to come take care of my baby boy."

Gabe wagged his tail and wriggled his body happily, letting her know he was just fine. She noticed a card on the kitchen table which confirmed Ann's visit. She was such a thoughtful person, always making her family and friends feel special.

Chloe walked over to the table and smiled when she saw Ann's handwriting scrawled across the envelope. She tore it open and smiled at the front of the card. It was a picture of her other favorite guy — Donald Duck. Donald wore a sad face and the inside of the card explained the expression with a message about how much she was missed.

Chloe hadn't been able to stop at the bagel store the last few mornings because she had been running later than usual after her late-night dates with Brian. She knew she needed to get back to her regular schedule. It kept her focused and close to her good friends like Greg and Ann. She knew better than to get swept away at the beginning of a relationship. It was important for her to keep her sense of self and stick to her routine. Maybe she wouldn't give

Brian a ring tonight, she thought to herself, as she made her way back over to the door and put on Gabe's leash for his walk.

She moved robotically through her usual nightly routine. When she was done with her chores, she picked up the phone and punched in Grace's number. After two rings, she answered.

"Hey, it's me," Chloe said as she settled down into her couch ready to chat with her best friend and enjoy the view of the Gulf out the sliding glass doors that wrapped around the side of her apartment. The candles she had lit filled her place with the delicious smell of an ocean breeze. She couldn't have been more content.

"Hey stranger, how are you?" Grace replied. "I'm not used to only talking to you once a week."

"I've been running around like crazy, spending a lot more time out than in, even when I'm not at work. I'm sorry I haven't called sooner. Gabe is upset with me, too. He barked me the riot act when I got home."

"I'm just kidding with you, sweetie. I figured you would be busy with the aftermath of your friend's murder. Not to mention your new love interest. I've been dying to hear whether anything has developed with the detective."

"I don't even know where to begin."

"Tell me the whole story. It has been years since I went on a date. I desperately need to live vicariously through you."

"Brian and I seem to be caught up in a whirlwind of emotions." Chloe went on to recount the whole week to Grace: the dates, the attraction, the news about his past and the progress with Molly's murder case. She was even more exhausted when she finished the tale than when she arrived home.

"Wow!" Grace said, sounding dumbstruck. "I don't even know where to begin. So much has happened in just one short week. Your life has changed, Chloe, unexpectedly. Everything changes when you get into a relationship. It sounds like he could be the one. I know that might sound corny, and it's probably too soon to tell, but I have a strong feeling that you've found the love of your life."

"Grace, do you really think so? You know, I felt the same thing from the first moment he smiled at me, but I don't want to be naive. Or get too hopeful. Since we went through it together, you know as well as I do that things haven't worked out for me in this area. It's all so scary. I don't think I could survive having my heart broken again, Grace. I don't think Brian would do such a thing, but I don't know if I can afford emotionally to take the risk. Life is good…I have a great dog, a beautiful apartment, an incredible job, wonderful friends and interesting hobbies. I don't want to mess things up. I'm scared, Gracie. It hit me on the drive home tonight. I suddenly realized that I had already fallen hard for a man I just met. I don't know what to do. I promised myself I wouldn't call him this evening so I would have a chance to clear my head. So, I called you instead."

"Chloe, my dear. Take a breather. I promise that it's all going to work out this time. You have been through so much, and you have always survived, come out on top in fact. Your challenges have made you so strong, so colorful with character. You are a beautiful person, inside and out. You deserve every happiness you can find in this world. I know you are scared. But you can't run away from this opportunity. An opportunity that has literally come to you. An opportunity that you didn't go out and look for.

She continued, with each bit of sage advice soothing Chloe's fears, "How can you turn it down if you don't first give it a chance? Your life crossed paths with Brian's for a reason. I know that you believe that as strongly as I do. Your strength, independence and your perseverance to create such a wonderfully rich life for yourself are the reasons that the door has opened for this man to come inside. It has always been important to you that you share your life with a special partner, have a family together. Don't deny yourself what has been presented to you so unexpectedly. The greatest gifts in life often come without warning, all the more special when they take us by surprise."

Chloe listened carefully as Grace spoke out loud what she already knew in her heart. For some reason, she just needed to hear these things from someone else. And not just from anyone else, either, but from her oldest and dearest friend in the world.

She let Grace continue on — thankful she had so much to say. Thankful she had such a spirit sister, someone who understood her so completely and supported her unconditionally. Grace's encouragement meant everything in the world to Chloe, and she soaked up her words that were a wonderful gift being showered over her. Grace's understanding washed away her fears and fueled her determination to make all of this work.

"Chloe, just give him a chance. That is all I ask of you. If you continue to give him a chance, I know that it will all work out. I promise you. And I don't hand out promises lightly."

"Everything you said is correct, Gracie. I already knew all of it in my heart. But sometimes I worry that I make too many decisions with my heart rather than my head."

"That is what makes you so special, Chloe. You are a sentimentalist. You make decisions with your heart because you live and love passionately. It is your dedication to everything you believe in, your determination to accomplish all that you set out to do that places you in a league of your own. Sets you apart from others. Don't ever doubt yourself, Chloe. You are perfect just the way you are, and it sounds like Brian might be just the man to realize that you are the most wonderful woman in the world."

"Only second to you, my ever-faithful, best friend."

Gabe startled both women as he barked furiously at something outside.

"What is Gabe barking at? Is everything okay?"

"I think everything is fine, though I'm not sure," Chloe said, trying to be brave but not sure she could convince Grace or herself of that. "Let me take a peek out the window."

Gabe continued his ranting as Chloe got off the couch to sneak a peek out her front window. As she peered out the slats of her Venetian blinds, the front doorbell rang, and she almost jumped out of her skin. She shrieked like a frightened child and scared Grace half to death.

"Chloe, it's me…Brian. I'm so sorry I scared you."

Chloe swallowed hard and pushed down the knot of emotions that had begun to develop in her stomach.

"Gracie, I'm going to have to finish this up tomorrow night. Brian is at my front door."

"I hope his ears weren't ringing from us talking about him," Grace laughed.

"I don't know, but I'll fill you in on everything tomorrow night. Keep me in your prayers, please. I need all the positive thoughts you can remember to send my way."

Chloe opened the front door and motioned for Brian to come in. She still had the phone glued to her ear.

"Not only do I believe that the two of you have a future as a couple, Chloe, I also think that you are going to solve this murder together. You will be a 'dynamic duo' — a formidable team."

Chloe watched as Gabe sniffed Brian up and down. She said goodbye to Grace and promised to call around the same time the next evening.

Brian bent down to greet Gabe on a dog-friendly level and looked up to talk with Chloe.

"Hi! I hope it's okay that I stopped by tonight. I won't even try and make up an excuse. I just wanted to see you."

Chloe smiled, letting him see she was very happy he had made the decision to visit her. The fact that he was comfortable enough to be so honest as to tell her his true motivation was very refreshing.

When Gabe was finished with his greeting, Brian stood up and gave Chloe a brief hug and then a kiss. Which led to another kiss. And soon they were passionately kissing.

Caught up in the moment, they didn't notice Gabe's concern over the situation. When they stopped to look, it was clear that he wasn't sure if he was happy about there being a new man in his mother's life. When they saw his expression, they laughed and both bent down to pet him and give him reassurance that it was okay and that he was still top dog.

"I don't want us to get off on the wrong foot. I know how important he is to you, and I don't want him to get upset. You can tell he's a very special dog."

"That he is," Chloe said. "All of my dogs have been special. But Gabe is one-of-a-kind. He is my confidant and my best friend. He keeps me on my toes, always eager to enjoy life to the fullest. Dogs and dolphins are very much alike in that way, you know. They truly brighten the lives of those around them on a daily basis, and they don't even have to try…it just comes naturally to them. It's part of their spirit. I'm so blessed. My life is surrounded at home and at work with these beautiful animals. I start each day with Gabe's enthusiasm for life, and then I go to work, if you can call it that, and am surrounded by some of God's most amazing and energetic marine mammals. Then it's back home to my little angel here. He greets me each evening as if I am the most special person on Earth. We have so much fun together. I don't know what I'd do without him."

"Your love for Gabe and all of your dolphins is contagious, Chloe."

"You are very sweet, Brian. Thank you for your kindness," Chloe responded, feeling heat rise into her cheeks as she turned away.

"It's easy to be genuine with you, Chloe. From the moment we met, I felt at ease. I'm sure you noticed that I was a little shaky when we stepped down onto the dock the night of the murder, but you helped me feel at home in a place that was foreign to me. There was something in your eyes that night that told me I could trust you. That's probably why I shared the information about my past with you so freely and quickly."

"It's nice to finally meet a man who appreciates those qualities in me. In the past, I've felt as if those qualities have either freaked men out or mistakenly given them the idea that I could be easily manipulated. You are one-of-a-kind, too, you know. I knew it the moment you turned and smiled at me the night we met."

Chloe put her arms around his neck and kissed him tenderly. Her stomach once again felt as if butterflies had been let loose to fly. They held each other for a long, heartfelt embrace.

Like a tsunami, he had crashed into her life, sweeping her off her feet without warning.

As his strong hands massaged her back, she wondered to herself what the odds were that she would survive the strong pull of his mighty handsome wave. Gabe realized that this moment didn't include him, and he retreated to his doggy bed to curl up with his stuffed animals.

Neither knew how much time had floated by, but the sun had set, and it had become dark inside without the lights on. Chloe winked at Brian, and he flashed her one of his incredible smiles. "I don't have to be a real detective to figure out that I enjoy kissing you, Mr. White."

"And I you, but I think Gabe is feeling left out." Brian pointed to the perceptive pup who was pretending to sleep, but really had one eye open keeping watch on them.

"Hey, Gabe, baby. Let's have your bedtime snack." Chloe bent down and hugged and kissed him, trying to make sure he felt special. She hoped that Gabe and Brian would become best buddies. She didn't want her faithful poodle to feel neglected or resent the new man in her life.

"Come on, I'll make us all something to eat," offered Brian.

"That type of treatment might just spoil me," Chloe pointed out as she retrieved her frying pan from the drawer underneath the oven.

"Somehow or another, I think you would adjust to it," Brian gently teased as he smiled warmly in her direction. "You take care of everyone else, Chloe. It's about time you let someone take care of you."

"Thanks, sweetie, for making me feel so special. If you just give me some time, I'm sure I could adjust to your TLC."

She went to the fridge and grabbed two eggs to make for Gabe. She called Gabe over and let him smell the eggs before she cracked them open, a little ritual of theirs. She turned to crack them and found that Brian had already started to heat the water for mac & cheese spirals. He took the eggs from her hands.

"Let me take care of those. How does he like them?"

"Scrambled is perfect. Let me just spray the pan for you first. You know, I said it would take a while for me to get used to being spoiled."

"It's never too early to start getting used to it," he pointed out. "Sit down and take it easy. I'll take care of everything, even the drinks. So don't go near that fridge."

"This is painful," Chloe remarked. "I'm not used to such treatment."

"Well, get used to it. There's a lot more to come."

Chloe left Gabe to beg for his eggs. Actually, he sat quietly and waited patiently for Brian to make their meal.

She sat down on the couch and looked for something entertaining on the TV. Pulling up a t-shirt memory quilt handmade by her aunt, added to her comfort. She loved to get warm and cozy curled up on the couch, and nothing made her feel as cozy as one of her quilts. Because her apartment was open between the kitchen, living room and dining room, she could see Brian and Gabe from the couch. She loved the flow of the space. It had a Florida feeling which made her right at home. She watched as Brian looked around, found Gabe's bowl and spooned the eggs into it. That sweet moment also made her feel right at home.

"You can use a drop of the spring water to help cool it off," she called over to him.

Gabe watched carefully as Brian fetched the water from the fridge and poured a little into his dog bowl. Brian then took the bowl and placed it on the bone-shaped place mat where he had originally found the dish. A water bowl was still in place on the mat, but Gabe found no interest in it. He sat right on cue and allowed Brian to serve him his eggs. As soon as his bowl hit the ground, he started to gobble them down.

Chloe smiled at the scene and knew Gabe would be happy with the double-egg treat. She hoped it would start his relationship with Brian on the right foot. The best way to Gabe's heart was always through his stomach. The boy loved his food. There was no question about that!

"He's happy now," she called over. "You have instantly made it to the top of his favorite person list."

"He really loved those eggs, huh? I've never seen anything like it. He's licking the bowl so tenderly, making sure he's gotten every last bite."

Brian laughed out loud at the sight of Gabe eating his egg snack. His smile stretched clear across his face, and Chloe couldn't help but smile as well. She was happy to see that he got as much of a kick out of Gabe as she did.

Brian finished up in the kitchen and brought the mac & cheese over to the coffee table.

"Is it okay if we eat here?"

"Of course it is. To tell you the truth, I eat here all the time."

Chloe set out a couple of coasters decorated with a pair of diving dolphins and took the iced teas from Brian to place upon them. Brian placed her bowl into her hands and set a bag of chips between them. He sat down next to her on the couch, and she reached over to spread the quilt across his lap as well. Before they knew it, Gabe had managed to jump up on and find a place to sit between the two of them. He never missed an opportunity to share a meal.

"Be careful, Brian. Gabe is very quick, and he thinks he's a person. He would have no problem helping himself to your food." As if on cue, Gabe reached over and gently snatched the chip that Brian was holding in his hand.

Brian looked down amazed. "Wow! He is fast. I didn't even see him make a move. Smart dog. He must have known I was an easy victim."

"He's just breaking you in. Amazingly enough, he still gets by me sometimes. He's slick when it comes to food. He makes me laugh all the time. I count my blessings every day that he's in my life. I can't imagine my life without a French masterpiece."

"You're a funny one, Chloe Martin."

"How am I funny? I'm just sitting here eating mac & cheese."

"You know what I mean," Brian chided her as he reached over and tickled underneath her chin in a light-hearted manner."

"Hey, those are dolphin tickles!"

"Dolphin tickles?"

"Yes, dolphin tickles. The dolphins love it when we tickle underneath their lower jaw, on their neck. They find it very silly. I'm a little scared, though. It seems as if I've already got you living in my fantasy world of poodles and dolphins!"

"I like your fantasy world."

"Me, too. I wish I could stay in it forever. Though we all know that's not possible. Which reminds me," she said as she straightened up on the couch. "I need to talk to you about the case."

"Hey. Let me enjoy this fantasy evening just a little longer, please. I'm not ready to talk about serious matters yet," he pleaded.

"Okay. As long as we talk about it at some point this evening. It may be important," Chloe added in so as to catch his attention.

"Now, you've piqued my curiosity. And you knew you would. You know you can't bring up a case and then expect me to wait on a piece of information that could possibly break it wide open."

"Good, because I've been excited about sharing this information with you all evening."

Brian leaned over and kissed her on the lips. It was a long, sensual kiss followed by a long moment of silence.

"Stop distracting me!" Chloe demanded. "I'm going to share my findings with you whether you like it or not!"

"You are right. The case needs to be our focal point. What can you tell me, my little detective?"

"I'm not sure I like your tone. I'm not a 'little detective.' In fact, it seems as if I'm in possession of the most pertinent information related to our case at this point."

"Our case? I didn't know you were employed by the Lee County Police," he teased her.

"Just a figure of speech. I know I'm not officially on the case, but I just can't leave it alone. I feel a responsibility to Molly to figure out who murdered her and why. Over the last few days, her presence has been around me, as if she's trying to help me figure things out."

"I was just playing with you, honey. I appreciate your help and respect your dedication to your colleague. You are a good person, dolphin girl. And a tad mysterious. Now tell me what you know!"

"It's really not that much new information, mainly gossip from the meeting tonight and a lead that might focus us in the right direction."

"Us, huh?" Brian teased as he playfully tickled her.

"Yes, us. Though I'm not sure I want to be your partner if you're going to act this way," Chloe shot back to let him know she could give as well as take.

"Oh, come on, Chloe. I'm sorry. You know I was just joking with you."

With that, he took her right hand and gently kissed the top of it. Sort of a Cinderella and Prince Charming kiss. He flashed her his broad smile, dimples and all, with the overall effect of melting her heart.

"What an apology! Totally unnecessary since I did know you were kidding, but I loved it nonetheless! I'm sure that little act has worked beautifully on all of your girlfriends."

"I've never tried it on anyone else. You're the first. I guess you inspired me!"

"Oh please, let's not get too over the top here. Do you want to hear what I have to contribute or not?"

"Of course! Enlighten me. I'm just a lowly detective who has never solved a case on his own."

"I'm sure it was difficult before you met me. I know you have a partner and all, but this crime stuff really intrigues me. I think I've watched every show out there, at least once, that deals with solving a crime. I loved watching *Murder She Wrote* when I was growing up, and I even took a Criminology class in college. But I digress. Let me get to the good stuff.

"First, Shannon and Theresa decided to call an emergency staff meeting tonight to discuss new security measures at the facility, and they managed to make quite a spectacle of themselves."

"How so?"

"Well, it seemed as if Shannon just didn't want to be at the meeting, at all. She was antsy from the beginning and downright rude when I held up the end of the meeting to ask a question and make a comment."

"How was she rude?"

"Well, she practically threw a temper tantrum. She really wanted to make the meeting short and get out of there. She asked if anyone had a question, but she said it in such a way as to get the message across that she really didn't want anyone to speak up."

"So, you decided to speak up anyway, I take it."

"Exactly! I didn't want to miss the opportunity while the whole staff was together. When I raised my hand to speak, she almost bit my head off. Theresa had to put her in her place. It was quite a show and very uncomfortable for all of the staff members. Shannon is usually the more laid-back sister, so it was out of character for her to get cranky. Since she doesn't take her work too seriously, she is often more fun to be around than Theresa. She loves the dolphins and the facility, but her family always comes first."

She continued, getting more worked up as she relayed her concerns, "She is the polar opposite of Theresa. Dolphin Connection *is* Theresa's family. Theresa and I have gotten along beautifully all these years because she respects hard work and rewards it. We relate to one another as perfectionists, workaholics and dedicated employees. She was visibly agitated when Shannon lashed out at me for delaying the close of the meeting. More than that, I think she appeared downright embarrassed by her sister's behavior. Since the meeting was held after hours without additional compensation, Shannon's behavior was even more out of line."

"Anyone who has worked a job that involves long hours for little pay would agree with that point," Brian noted sincerely.

"She would have done herself a big favor if she hadn't huffed and puffed while I talked," Chloe continued, having caught her breath when Brian chimed in. "Innocently, I reached out to ask for the help of anyone at Dolphin Connection who may have known if something was troubling Molly. Then I offered to be in charge of setting up a memorial to honor her memory. Like most things, if someone doesn't take responsibility for a project, it falls by the wayside. It would be a travesty for Molly's time at Dolphin Connection to go unnoticed."

"That's generous of you to offer your already limited time to make the memorial happen. It's important to honor those who have been taken needlessly. It's the wish of this detective that each murder victim whose death I investigate be remembered in a special way. Especially when it seems that nobody outside of The Department cares what truly happened to them. It would be unimaginable to go through life without people who cared enough to miss you if you were gone."

"We are both fortunate to have such people in our lives, including each other," Chloe said, straight from her heart and soul.

"Molly has a lot of people who care about her as well. At least once a day, I hear from her parents regarding the investigation. They are putting a lot of pressure on us to figure out just what happened at Dolphin Connection the evening she was murdered and to bring her killer to justice."

"That's good that her family is involved. I would like to meet them someday. Do they plan on coming down to the area?"

"They initially came down to identify her body and then returned home. They are currently waiting for her body to be ready for release from the CSI Department, which should be any day now. They will then come back to clean out her apartment, collect her belongings from Dolphin Connection and escort her body home. Some of her things are being held as evidence at this point. Those items will have to be returned to her family at a future date."

"Did you find anything interesting at the apartment or in her office at Dolphin Connection? I'm assuming you were able to go through her desk and her files at work."

"We went through everything, but none of it looked curious to me. She did, however, have files upon files that told about the life history of each dolphin. She seemed to be paying particular attention to the family heritage of each dolphin as that information was highlighted for each animal in her notes."

"That's interesting. I didn't know Molly was researching the lineage of each dolphin quite that closely and extensively. She must have been particularly interested in breeding practices," Chloe said, remembering that Molly's Research Seminar notes also indicated a little bit of that, but certainly not to the extent Brian had discovered.

"Is that important?"

"Well, breeding practices are sort of a hot button topic among dolphin facilities today."

"How come?" Brian asked.

"Since the Marine Mammal Protection Act of 1972, it has been illegal to collect marine mammals from the wild. This means that modern facilities grow their dolphin families when they have offspring born to their present dolphins, receive a dolphin from another facility or nurse back to health a sick, injured or stranded animal from the wild who would no longer be able to survive in the wild if returned there. The first of these practices is most popular since it is most predictable. The problem is that all facilities have a limited gene pool. It's important that male dolphins do not mate with their female offspring and so on and this issue greatly limits the number of dolphins who can mate. As time creeps forward, a facility's gene pool becomes tighter and tighter. Some facilities have even started loaning each other their male dolphins for a year or two at a time in order to expand their gene pools. While it's often used for humans with infertility issues, artificial insemination can aid marine mammal breeding practices by widening the gene pool if the sperm can safely travel in a timely manner to the intended female dolphin."

"That all makes sense. The whole topic is interesting and something I probably never would have known about if I hadn't met you, Chloe Martin!"

"I'm glad I could be of service to you, Detective White. All this teaching has more than tired me out, though, and I need to walk Gabe and get some rest."

"One more thing before we say goodnight. Do you think that Molly could have ruffled somebody's feathers if she was looking into the breeding practices at Dolphin Connection with such passion?"

"Definitely. It's a very sensitive subject matter and one that is handled only at the top by Shannon and Theresa. Even senior trainers like myself and heads of departments are not consulted in decisions having to do with breeding practices."

"How can we find out more about what Molly was up to in her short time at Dolphin Connection?"

"I've already set up a meeting for tomorrow evening with one of the girls from the Education Department. She reviewed the Research Seminar with Molly when she first arrived and can possibly point out the changes Molly made to the program. Understanding Molly's frame of mind and focus during her time at Dolphin Connection should help point us in the direction of why she was murdered. If there is one thing I know for sure it's that Molly's death wasn't an accident. She was killed to be silenced. I'm feeling it deep in my bones."

"I agree," Brian said, "There's something fishy going on at Dolphin Connection that we haven't figured out yet. Hopefully, the meeting tomorrow night will be helpful."

"Definitely. The staff member we are meeting with has been at the facility even longer than me, and she is a dear friend. She wants to help us for all the right reasons. There is no doubt in my mind, however, that she will also find time to check up on you while she's helping us. Consider this fair warning. Rest assured, I already told her you are a good catch!"

"A *good* catch?!"

"Okay, I told her you're a great catch!"

"Thanks for all your help, Chloe. I really appreciate it. Maybe you should be getting paid by The Department!"

"I'll settle for getting paid with more of your kisses and maybe a foot rub! I could fetch you some lotion to use that will leave my feet and your hands smelling like we just took a walk on the beach! You'll have to use your imagination for the gentle, lapping sounds of the waves and the romantic glow of the moonlight…"

"It's easy to use my imagination when I'm with you, dolphin girl!"

Chapter 20

Chloe awoke to Brian quietly slipping off the couch before the sun had even come up. She couldn't tell what time it was or how long they had slept. Never turned off, the TV was blaring with an early morning infomercial. All she could remember was that first Brian had taken Gabe for his midnight walk and then he had returned to give her the most relaxing foot and leg rub of her life. She had melted into sleep on the couch.

"Hey, where are you going so early?" She asked.

"I tried to be so careful. I'm sorry I woke you up," he said, leaning down to kiss the top of her head.

"I'm an amateur sleuth, remember? You can't just sneak out of my apartment without me noticing!"

"I wasn't sneaking out on you, dolphin girl. I've got to get to the office early this morning. No reason for both of us to suffer. Our conversation about Molly's work at Dolphin Connection kept me tossing and turning all night. It was as if we discovered some big clue, but we just don't fully realize it yet. I think we are getting closer to figuring out just what happened last Wednesday night."

"Is there anything more I can do to help you?" Chloe asked.

"Just get some more sleep. It's only 4 AM."

"So that's why it's still pitch dark out and Gabe hasn't even stirred."

“Listen, have a great day and keep those plans with your friend for tonight. Maybe she can help us figure out what is bothering me. Where and when do you want to meet her?”

“Let’s say 7 PM at her place. I’ll text you her address. Eliza said she’d pick up pizza and soda, and I’ll grab dessert. I’d rather not meet at a restaurant and have other people hear our conversation.”

“Good point. Is there anything I can bring?”

“Just yourself, sweetie. And any information you think might help us figure out this mess.”

“Then seven it is. Forget the text, I’ll pick you up here, and we can head over to Eliza’s place together. OK?”

“I can’t wait. Have a wonderful day and don’t miss me too much!”

“Aren’t you full of yourself at such an early hour of the morning! But you are right. I will miss you!”

He leaned over and gave her a gentle hug and kiss goodbye.

Before he could make a quick escape, she called out to him. “What kind of pizza do you like?”

“If you are such a great detective, then why can’t you figure that one out on your own?”

“I’d take you for a pepperoni, black olive and mushroom guy.”

Brian’s mouth fell open and his jaw dropped.

“How in the world did you know that?”

“Just a lucky guess,” she said in amazement at how good she was getting with her secret talents. “A natural observation of sorts. You enjoyed all three of those ingredients when we ate Italian food the other night.”

“A keen eye. You amaze me, dolphin girl!”

“It interests me to make note of the details in my world,” she responded. “And sometimes, I just seem to sense things. I'm not sure what that is all about, though! Crazy, I know, but it seems to be getting stronger with age."

Brian walked across the room and gave her another kiss. This time it was a sensual, heated kiss that made her want him to stay much longer.

"Don't start something you don't intend to finish," she teased as she playfully pushed him away.

Brian stopped and looked thoughtfully into her sleepy eyes. "I think I'm falling in love with you, Chloe Martin. I didn't think I'd ever feel this way about someone again. This certainly has been a whirlwind romance."

"You take my breath away, Detective White. But, I think you're just bringing up that love thing because I'm helping you solve your case!" She added in a joking manner. "Now get out of here and make me proud by solving this crime."

Brian looked a little hurt as he kissed her goodbye again and headed for the door. Chloe knew exactly why and summoned up all of her courage.

"Hey, Detective!"

"Yes." He stopped in the doorway and turned to face her.

"I'm falling in love with you, too."

He flashed her one of his broad smiles, dimples and all, and nodded to let her know that was exactly what he needed to hear.

"Now get out of here. You've already made me spill my guts and now I feel totally vulnerable. I promised myself I would never let myself be in this position again."

He walked back to her and held her for a long time in his arms. Finally, he let her go, pushed back and looked straight in her eyes. "You can trust me, Chloe. I know you've been hurt deeply in the past, but I intend never to let that happen to you again. I've been hurt, too, but I trust you. For some reason, I know in my heart that this is the real thing. It's like I knew you before I met you. You are the woman I've been looking for my whole life, and I feel incredibly lucky that our lives have come together so unexpectedly."

"Destiny. I've believed in it since I was a little girl. It's what has gotten me through the rough times — the knowledge that everything always works out the way it's supposed to in the end. I thought my chance to meet the right person had passed a long time ago. And then there you were, out of the blue. When you turned to introduce yourself that first night, it was magical. Somehow, I knew you were the one, my soul mate. The other half I never thought I would find."

"I felt exactly the same way. It was so strange because I'm usually all business on the job, especially at a crime scene. But when I turned and saw you, my breath was taken away. I hope I didn't fumble over my words too much. I was trying to still be professional."

"Don't worry. I was busy being distracted by the butterflies in my stomach and the fireworks in my head. Strange doesn't come close to covering it. Within minutes, I went from being scared to death at seeing the most horrible thing I've ever witnessed in my life to being totally overcome by you. Guilt ran through me knowing that Molly's cold body was only a stone's throw away, while chills ran up and down my spine as you smiled at me. It's ironic that such a tragic even brought us together. Life seems to go that way, though. At least my life does. It's basically a series of ironies. God certainly must have some sense of humor. I'm sure there's a plan behind everything that happens, but I can't seem to figure it out. You took my statement when we met. I called Grace that evening and mentioned you. Then I didn't think about you again until The Hurricane."

"You didn't think about me, at all? I couldn't stop thinking about you…to the point that I was having a hard time concentrating on the investigation. I even told my partner that I'd met 'the love of my life.' Though I didn't tell him it was the woman who had found the murdered body at the dolphin facility."

"The day following the murder was jam packed because I picked up Molly's responsibilities with the Dolphin Learners' Group. By the time I ran into my old college boyfriend, Todd, on one of the morning dolphin tours, it had already been a wild day. It was all just too much at the moment, and I was wobbly on my feet. Finding Molly's body the night before and then running into him. I couldn't imagine why God was giving such a heavy load to bear in such a short amount of time. Pulling it together and digging deep made it possible to finish out the work day. The Hurricane is my favorite restaurant, and so Bailey and I planned to meet there at our regular table, a perk because we enjoy being regulars. As fate would have it, Todd was there, too. When it became apparent he still had a wandering eye, I suddenly realized that my life had turned out exactly as it was meant to. Once and for all, I let him go. Bailey arrived, and we had a great dinner. When I bumped into you, all those feelings from the night before rushed over me."

"It does make sense," Brian chimed in. "In order to be ready to start over, you needed to be confronted with your past."

Chloe said, "When I collided with you that evening, I was ready to start over. To take another chance at love. I hadn't really bothered much in the years since Todd and I broke up. My life was the dolphins and Gabe. The risk of getting hurt again wasn't an option. They say you only risk what you know you can survive losing, and I knew I couldn't lose another partner. Until I met you, I wasn't ready."

"I wasn't ready, either. The all-encompassing nature of my job has kept me fulfilled and grounded until now. All in God's perfect timing," Brian replied.

"There have been times I've wished God would hurry up on the timing issue! Though if this came into place sooner, much of my extra time with the dolphins due to my single lifestyle would have been missed. Hindsight really is 20/20, but it's so hard to trust, isn't it? Even when I remind myself that things eventually work out in the end, I get stressed out until they do."

"We are all human. Most of us don't really believe things until we see them unfold in plain sight," Brian offered. "Until we have physical proof…and not just hope. Belief and hope are abstract. Faith is difficult because it's not concrete, either. Most of us mortals need results before we have faith. Full reliance on God; now there's a challenge."

"Stop!" Chloe crowed. "How did we get from feelings to faith in the blink of an eye?!"

"Because they are inextricably tied together. Whether we want to believe it or not."

"You have a point there, Detective White. There really are no concrete answers to these matters. So, let's leave it at that! Faith is a personal matter, a lifelong challenge to develop."

Brian responded, "Very true, but it's interesting to philosophize, dolphin girl. I love having these long discussions with you!"

"Long is right. You know 3 hours have passed since you were first going to leave."

"Crap! I've got to get to the office. You are quite a distraction," Brian said.

He leaned over, gave her a quick kiss and exited her apartment.

"I'll see you at 7 PM," she called after him.

"See you then. I'll bring some wine in case anyone wants a drink."

"Great!" She replied.

Chloe stretched, rolled off the couch and quickly got dressed. She pulled on her shorts and a Dolphin Connection tank top. The shirt was her favorite, a pretty, pale pink with a picture of a female dolphin and her two young calves jumping in the waves underneath script letters that spelled Dolphin Connection. She'd bought the top when she was an intern at Dolphin Connection many years earlier, and it always made her smile when she wore it.

She loved the picture of the mother and her twins because of the rarity of a dolphin having a successful multiple birth. Her top reminded her that things did happen in life even when they were greatly against the odds. There it was again…Full Reliance on God. FROG — for short!

Gabe got up, stretched and shook. Knowing that it concluded with him polishing off a delicious breakfast, he was ready to take care of the rest of the morning routine efficiently. A quick walk gave Chloe just enough time to stop for her morning bagel. She kissed Gabe on his snout, made him grunt with a bear hug and headed to NY Bagels for a short visit with Greg and Ann.

Chapter 21

"Hi Greg! Hi Ann! How is everyone today?" Chloe swung open the door to her favorite bagel store and greeted her old friends with a big smile.

"Well, there she is! Look who has finally gotten in to see us! I like seeing your face in person, Chloe, rather than receiving a phone call saying that you won't be in again. Though, thanks as always for staying in touch. I'd worry if you didn't call," remarked Greg.

"I know you would, Greg, and I'm sorry I haven't been in as much lately. Things have been so hectic since the murder at Dolphin Connection last week."

Chloe noticed the ears of the customers in the store perk-up when she mentioned murder and Dolphin Connection in the same sentence, and she decided she better shut her mouth quickly. Luckily, Ann came out from behind the bagel bins to greet her and managed to change the conversation.

"I think something more than that is going on here, Greg. Look at our girl! She is glowing like crazy. I know that glow! Chloe Martin, you are in love."

Chloe blushed so readily she gave herself away.

"I knew it, I knew it. Greg, bring Chloe's breakfast over to our table." Ann took Chloe by the arm and escorted her to a nearby table where they both sat down. "Now, tell me all about this new love in your life. How long have you been dating? Is he cute? Is he husband material? Father material? What does he do for a living? Oh my God, I'm so excited for you, I could just burst!"

"Slow down, Ann, slow down. Why don't I start with your last question first because it's the reason we met at all. Brian, that's his name, Brian White, is a detective for the local police department. We met last Wednesday night when he was called on the scene at Dolphin Connection to investigate Molly Green's murder. Since I was the one who found Molly's body, Brian and I met shortly after he arrived. He interviewed me and then let me go home after one of my bosses arrived. Then I bumped into him the following evening at The Hurricane, and the rest is history. He is a real sweetheart, very smart and very handsome. Definitely husband and father material. We've only know each other for a week, but I believe in my heart he's the one for me."

"Oh, Chloe, I'm so happy for you! I've been hoping and praying this day would come. I'm sure we both would have preferred it come sooner rather than later, but it sounds like he was worth waiting for!"

"Definitely worth waiting for, that's for sure! The events of the last week have convinced me that everything comes at the right time. Sometimes, we just have to wait longer than we'd like for the things that are most important to us," Chloe said.

"I don't know how you always see things so clearly, young lady. You are wise beyond your years."

"I'm an old soul, Ann. When it's not your first time around, you start out ahead of the game."

They laughed together as this wasn't the first time Chloe had shared her belief about being an old soul with her dear friend.

"You know," Ann said, "I've never believed much in that 'old soul' stuff, but in your case, it really does seem to explain things."

Greg appeared at the table and since there was nobody in line, at least at the moment, he joined the ladies at the table.

"Now bring me up to date, ladies," he instructed as he took his seat. "I want to know everything."

"Since I was already running late when I arrived, I need to eat my breakfast in order to make it to work on time. Ann, you'll have to fill him in for me, please," Chloe said.

"My pleasure, Chloe."

Ann filled Greg in on the details of Chloe's love life and beamed as she told the story. They were more like proud parents than close friends.

"Well, we're going to have to meet this man soon. We wouldn't want you going and falling in love before we make sure he is good enough for you," Greg said.

Everyone laughed, and Chloe nodded her head. Not only were Ann and Greg like proud parents, they were protective as well.

"How about tomorrow night, Chloe? Ann and I would love to treat you and Brian to a fancy dinner. We can all get dressed up and share a fine dining experience together. Brian will be so busy enjoying the wonderful food and drink, he won't even realize we're checking him out!"

"You're too much, Greg. Let me talk to him tonight and see if Friday evening works for him. I'll stop by on the way to work in the morning to firm things up. Now, I better hit the road and fast. I've never been late to work in my life, and I'm not going to break that record now." Chloe pushed back her chair, threw her aqua, shell-motif Vera Bradley backpack over her shoulder and grabbed her tray. "Love you both. I'll see you in the morning."

As she made a quick exit, a line of customers filed up to the counter and Greg and Ann rushed back to their posts.

Chloe dashed across the street and just missed getting hit by a car that was driving through the parking lot way too fast. She took a deep breath after the close call and took a moment to thank her guardian angel who was always looking out for her. She jumped in her car, backed out slowly and headed for Dolphin Connection. Though she was short on time, she knew it was better to drive safely than speed and have an accident.

She turned on the radio and flipped through the stations. Frustrated that there wasn't any good music to be found, she pulled out one of her favorite CDs. She loved to listen to Broadway show tunes. They reminded her of growing up near NYC. She popped *Hamilton* into the CD player and turned up the volume. She belted out the words to her favorite musical, words she knew backwards and forwards.

She was on top of the world. She just couldn't believe how well things were going between she and Brian. Lost in her dreamy thoughts and her off-key vocals, she almost drove right by the entrance to Dolphin Connection.

She gasped as she suddenly realized that she was practically on top of the huge dolphin sculpture that marked the parking lot of her facility. She pulled a quick right and then had to jam on her brakes to avoid hitting a family of tourists who were crossing the parking lot and heading for the entrance to Dolphin Connection.

"Oh shoot!" She exclaimed. "That's my second close call in a matter of fifteen minutes! What is going on here?"

She took another deep breath as she pulled into her parking space and turned off her Mustang. She thanked her guardian angel once again for saving her hide and grabbed her bag on the seat next to her. She hadn't the time to put the top down on her Mustang that morning so she was able to make a fast exit from the car. She slammed the door shut and locked the car, though it was totally unnecessary and simply an old habit from growing up in New York.

She headed for the employee gate with laser focus. Halfway there, she remembered that staff members were no longer allowed to enter through that gate and made an about face and headed for the gift shop main entrance. She got caught up in the midst of a throng of guests who had arrived at the facility with great anticipation of their dolphin swims.

She squeezed her way around the line that had formed to sign in at the front desk and scanned the shop to see if any new dolphin merchandise had arrived since she last checked. She loved to use her employee discount and noticed a great new sweatshirt — one with a mother and two calves, just like her tank top, and made a mental note to return later to buy it.

Chloe had noticed a large black cloud on her way from the car and feared the day might not be as bright as she had originally felt, especially after her two close calls. The sweatshirt was a positive omen, and it made her feel lighter again and excited to spend the day with her dolphin friends. With a joyous heart, she pushed on the handle of the back door and had just stepped through the opening when she heard her name being called across the gift shop. Sue, the Manager, was waving her arms and beckoning her to come back inside.

When Chloe turned around and let the back door close behind her, Sue came running across the shop and stopped directly in front of her with great urgency. She couldn't believe Sue had left a long line of guests at the front desk and made such a spectacle of herself. She was usually quite professional. Her odd behavior brought a sudden alarm and trepidation that Chloe felt in the pit of her stomach. The black clouds, maybe they had meant something.

"Chloe, I can't believe I almost missed you. I was so busy with the guests, I didn't even see you pass through. It's been so busy this morning with all of the staff members having to use the gift shop entrance."

"Sue, slow down. Why did you call me back into the shop? Has something happened?"

"When Shannon came in this morning, she gave me specific instructions to notify her of your arrival. She wants you to stay here until she comes to meet you."

"What are you talking about, Sue? I need to get to my office and check my schedule for any changes. My first session is in 15 minutes!"

"I'm just following directions, Chloe. I'm sorry. Shannon didn't tell me anything else. I'll go ahead and call to let her know you're here. I'm sure everything is fine, Chloe. Just wait in here, okay? I don't want any trouble with Shannon."

Sue leaned over and gave Chloe a quick hug before she headed back to her desk to make the aforementioned phone call. The guests were becoming visibly annoyed that Sue had left them waiting in line with no explanation for her absence. As she watched Sue pick up the phone, Chloe's heart sunk. Her stomach clenched tighter, and she broke out in a sweat.

"What could this possibly be about?" She blurted so loudly that a couple of the guests turned and looked at her sympathetically, having no difficulty seeing that she was visibly upset. She quickly began to realize that the two close calls and the black cloud were bad omens. The day that had started so magically with Brian had started to go downhill fast.

As she watched Shannon approach the back door to the gift shop, she couldn't believe the stern expression on her face. She looked mad as hell, as if she was going to burst.

Chloe started to shake, assuming the worst.

Chapter 22

"I've been fired."

"Chloe, is that you? What are you talking about, sweetie?" Brian asked, sounding as confused as she was.

"I've been fired. When I arrived at work this morning, I was instructed to wait in the gift shop until Shannon came to get me. When she arrived and instructed me to follow her to the main office, I knew it was over. When we reached her office, Theresa was already there waiting for us. They told me to sit down and curtly informed me that my services were no longer needed at Dolphin Connection. I almost fell off my chair as tears started to stream down my face. I turned to Theresa in disbelief, and she turned away from me. When I asked why, Shannon said that they were not obligated under Florida law to offer me an explanation. She then warned me that she would escort me to my desk to retrieve my belongings, and that I was not to say a word to any of my fellow staff members if I wanted to see any severance pay. It was an embarrassing walk of shame when she paraded me to my desk with a box in which I silently packed up my things. All those years' worth of memories that I had built up at the facility. The other trainers in the office at the time watched in shock and disbelief. I've never been so humiliated in my life. I couldn't believe what was happening, Brian. It felt as if I was having an out of body experience, looking down on myself, from far above unable to accept the reality of the situation."

“I am so sorry, Chloe. I can’t believe this has happened to you. Where are you now?” He asked.

“I’m home with Gabe. I had nowhere else to go.”

“Hang tight, dolphin girl. I’ll be right over. I promise this will be okay. They can’t get away with this, Chloe. If one of those sisters didn’t look guilty of murder before, they certainly do now. Especially since we can’t seem to uncover anyone else with a valid motive. Even Molly’s boyfriend Luke, who was a possible suspect due to their relationship, has been cleared. There is no real case against him. He definitely knows something he’s not telling us, though I started to doubt that he was actually involved in any foul play. If anything, it seems like he isn’t a criminal…just a loser. There seems to be more to this case than meets the eye. Shannon’s bizarre behavior at your staff meeting last night and your unexpected and unexplained termination from the facility where you have dedicated so many years of your life make her look very guilty. There is something one or both of those sisters don’t want us to know about, that’s for sure!”

“It must tie into something Molly discovered in her research efforts. She definitely uncovered something that is making both Shannon and Theresa very uncomfortable. Theresa wouldn’t even glance in my direction this morning. It was shocking that she could just sit there and allow Shannon to let me go with absolutely no explanation. Theresa has been my greatest supporter since I arrived at Dolphin Connection. None of this makes any sense. What am I going to do, Brian? The dolphins are such a huge part of my life. It’s like my children have been taken away from me. Thank God nobody can take Gabe. He is wrapped up in my arms right now, and I’m never going to let him go.”

“Everything is going to work out, Chloe. I promise. You will be back on the docks with your dolphins before you know it. We're getting closer to the truth. I'm sure of it. People naturally get nervous when you get too close to the truth."

"Are you almost here, sweetie?" She asked, needing his love and strong arms.

"Open up your front door. I'm just making my way up your stairs."

"We were so busy talking, Gabe and I didn't even hear your car."

"I'm a detective, remember? I'm supposed to be able to sneak up on you."

Chloe opened-up the front door, and Brian was standing in front of her.

They both turned off their phones, and Brian opened his arms wide. Chloe fell into him and was enveloped by his protective embrace. The tears she had held back earlier now flowed freely and heavily. He tightened his hold on her and simultaneously began to rub her back and assure her that he would take care of everything. Chloe opened her eyes and pushed back from his hold after a good, long cry that exhausted her.

The sun was bright and blinded her as she looked into it momentarily. The day that had begun bright and sunny had been interrupted by a terrible thunderstorm that was now followed by a gorgeous sky. She squinted her eyes and was amazed to see a double rainbow in the distance.

"Oh my God, Brian. Look! Look!"

"What is it?" He turned to look where she was pointing in a near hysteric state.

"Calm down, sweetie. It's just a rainbow."

"Actually, two rainbows," she noted. "Look again."

Brian looked up, and his face lit up when he spotted the beautiful art in the sky. "Rainbows are good luck, Chloe. I told you everything would be okay. More than just okay.

Things are going to turn out better than we expected. I promise."

Chloe looked into his eyes and knew he was right. Things were going to be fine. She also knew she could trust this man that stood before her.

"Rainbows are a positive sign, especially two of them. I have always believed strongly in signs, and this is definitely a good one. Thank you so much for coming over, Brian. I don't think I could have made it through this morning without knowing you were there to support me."

"You are a strong, independent woman, Chloe Martin. You are going to make it through this because of your inner strength and character. Just keep your eye on the prize and your faith with God. We must figure out who murdered Molly before this situation gets any messier. Sit down here in the warm sun, and I'll get us both some Snapple."

"Could you let Gabe out to sit with me, please?"

"Sure, dolphin girl. Just sit down and take it easy. Try to take some deep breaths. You don't want your body to take on too much stress. It's unhealthy."

"Yes, Doctor White," she joked.

"I'm glad to hear you still have your sense of humor." He smiled at her and headed inside. He let Gabe out to join her, as promised.

"Come on, Gabe," Chloe beckoned to her little angel. "Let's sit down together, Gabey."

Gabe trotted over and joined her on one of her comfortable porch chairs. She had splurged on the set because she spent so much time on the porch reading, writing and painting. The furniture set she had chosen was bamboo with overstuffed cushions decorated with palm trees. She sat in one of the two wave recliners that were incredibly comfortable. The table and chairs were a little stiffer, but perfect for lunches overlooking the Gulf and dinner parties with friends.

Brian walked over and handed her a raspberry flavored iced tea.

"Here we are. Don't you two look comfortable? Those chairs are great. This one right next to you seems to have my name on it."

"I knew there was a reason I bought two of them," she said.

"This view is incredible, Chloe. The water, the palm trees…it's truly paradise. It's clear to me why you love this place so much."

Tears began to stream down her face again. She just couldn't hold them back.

"Oh no, what have I said to upset you?" Brian asked.

He popped up from his wave chair, set his iced tea on the table in between them and sat on the edge of her chair so that he could hold her.

"It's not your fault, sweetie. It's just that when you mentioned how great this place is it made me realize that Gabe and I may not be able to live here much longer if I can't find a new job in the area. This is our home. We're not ready to leave it."

Gabe nodded his head in agreement right on cue.

"That's not going to happen, Chloe. The truth will surface soon, and you'll have your old job back. You're my dolphin girl! Nothing is going to change that. Nothing. Look at your shirt and remember your motivation," Brian reassured her.

"This is a very special shirt. I've had it for years, and it usually brings me good luck."

"The day is not over yet, Chloe. Sometimes really bad things end up having really good endings. What happened this morning is only going to bring us that much closer to

Molly's killer. My investigation is narrower now. In fact, it's going to be focused directly on Shannon and Theresa. They may think they solved their problem by firing you this morning, but their problems have only begun. One of them is guilty of murder, and the other knows more than she's willing to reveal. It's illegal to withhold evidence and information related to a crime, so both of them are guilty of something."

"Thanks for being so supportive. You should probably be heading back to work."

"Are you sure you'll be okay?" He asked.

"I'll be fine. Gabe is here to look after me. Right now, all I want to do is crawl into bed and pull my quilt over my head!"

"You should get some rest. Your mind and body need to process the stress you experienced this morning."

"We're still on for tonight, right?" She asked.

"Definitely. Would it help if I picked up the dessert so that you won't have to go out?"

"Absolutely not. It will give me something productive to do rather than just sitting around and feeling sorry for myself. Thanks for the offer, though," she replied.

"Let me know if you change your mind. You think your friend will still want us to show up, don't you?"

"She'll want us there early. She'll be so curious to find out what happened this morning, she'll be ready to explode. I haven't heard from any of my friends from Dolphin Connection yet, which can only mean that Shannon and Theresa threatened them with their jobs not to get in touch with me while they're at work. They don't know we are meeting with Eliza tonight. Besides, they can't tell her what she can or can't do on her own time."

"Very true. Though appropriate business etiquette doesn't seem to be of much concern to them right now."

"That's for sure," Chloe agreed.

Brian leaned over, kissed her and then pulled back. He gently held her chin in his right hand and looked straight into her eyes. A strand of her hair had fallen in front of her eyes, and he pushed it behind her ear with his left hand.

"Chin up, Chloe. I promise everything will work out. This will be the first of many promises I will make to you and keep during our life together."

"I trust you, Brian. I promise to hold it together and stay strong until this whole mess plays itself out."

"I'm going to run. I'll see you tonight." He got up from the chair and patted Gabe on his head. "Take care of my girl here until I can get back tonight."

To show that he understood, Gabe stood up and moved over to the space next to Chloe that Brian had vacated. He then proceeded to fall into Chloe's arms — his ultimate snuggle move.

"You're obviously in good hands, or should I say paws?"

"Gabe will take good care of me. Now you get going. We don't need you to lose your job, too!"

"Don't worry. That's not going to happen. Just take care of yourself today, Chloe."

"I will, I promise. By the way, I look forward to the lifetime of kept promises you mentioned earlier."

Brian flashed her his best smile yet and even blushed a little. "I'll see you tonight, love of my life."

As he began to take the steps down to his car, Chloe thought of something and popped up from her chair. She leaned over the railing and saw that she had caught him just before he got into his car. "Where are you heading?" She called down.

He looked up in her direction, obviously touched by her continued interest in his whereabouts and the case despite her horrible morning. "I'm heading to Dolphin Connection to have a conversation with two very suspicious sisters. If they thought they made your day unpleasant, they have no idea what they are in store for from me."

Chloe nodded with satisfaction, and Brian waved goodbye as he jumped into his car. She waved back and then turned and beckoned Gabe. "Let's go, buddy. We're crawling under the covers and hiding from this day for at least a little while."

Chloe let Gabe into their apartment, closed the door behind them and followed her poodle to their bedroom. Gabe jumped up on the bed, but Chloe hesitated before joining him.

Tears began to flow once again as she admired the beautiful quilt that graced her bed. The quilt was a labor of love done by her grandmother. The double Irish chain pattern was meant to bring luck. The fabrics were chosen with care to reflect Chloe's interest in everything marine. The result was a beautiful work of art that showed off fabrics with dolphins jumping and sea lions playing. The colors, from bright pinks to vibrant turquoises, were exquisite.

Chloe thought of her grandmother and how nice it would be to have her immediate family nearby at a time like this. It would be such a comfort. She rounded the end of the bed and crawled under the covers. Gabe nuzzled up next to her.

"Thank God for you and Brian, Gabe. This morning would have been unbearable without both of you." She hugged him, and he returned the show of affection by covering her face with tender kisses. Chloe looked at him and smiled, overcome with a sense of peace.

"Brian's right, buddy. I have no idea how, but everything is going to be okay."

Gabe gave her a final big kiss on the nose to show that he was in agreement.

She was so wound up with emotions, her nap didn't last long. She tried to sleep thinking that it might help her forget about her problems, but she had no such luck. She spent about an hour tossing and turning and then decided to call it quits. She threw back the quilt and realized that Gabe hadn't shared her difficulty falling asleep and was now thoroughly annoyed by her boisterous exit from bed.

"I'm sorry, Gabe. I didn't know you were sleeping. I couldn't hear you snoring with all of my tossing and turning. I'll fix the covers so that you can stay in bed and continue your nap."

He grunted in response and seemed to be content when Chloe remade the bed and placed a pillow next to him. He stood up, circled a few times, moved the quilt around a little bit with his mouth and paws and then curled up in a tiny ball wedged perfectly against the pillow. Chloe couldn't help but giggle at his ritual and noticed that she felt better as she let laughter wash over her.

She left the bedroom and went out to the kitchen for a snack. But when she arrived at the fridge, she decided she wasn't really hungry and closed the door after spending several minutes scanning the contents. She wandered into the living room, noticed her book on the coffee table and picked it up. She decided to sit out on the porch and read since it had turned out to be such a beautiful day, weather-wise.

She was reading an entertaining mystery by the daughter of a well-known writer, and she had been moving through it at a fast clip. This morning, however, she found herself reading lines over and over, and she had a hard time following the plot, which never happened. Usually she was ahead of the writer. Her head was spinning uncontrollably, and she just couldn't concentrate.

She got up from her lounge chair and headed back inside. She threw her book back on the coffee table and plopped on the couch. She grabbed the remote control, turned on the television and started to aimlessly flip through the channels. She finally found an old episode of *Matlock* and decided to leave it on. She watched as one of her favorite old-time actors, Andy Griffith, played the character of Ben Matlock, a defense lawyer who could swiftly get to the bottom of any crime.

"I wish Brian and I could solve the case of Molly's murder this easily," she blurted out loud, though there was no one in the room to hear her, not even Gabe.

Then maybe I could get my job back, she thought to herself. She was suddenly overwhelmed with terrible anxiety and tremendous sadness. She realized that if she and Brian couldn't figure out this mess, and she didn't get her job back, she may never see her dolphins or some of her colleagues again. She was set to have a final in-water session with the Dolphin Learner students that very day as part of their celebratory farewell, and now they would hear that she had been fired. The students wouldn't know her side of the story. She just hoped they wouldn't judge her too harshly.

Theresa and Shannon had made it explicitly clear that morning that she was not to step foot on the grounds of Dolphin Connection. That meant she would never see her dolphins again. Chloe couldn't bear to think of such a thing. The dolphins didn't know what happened. They would simply think she had abandoned them.

That last thought was the one that put her over the edge. At first, tears started to streak down her face and then her nose started to run. Within moments, she was crying and sobbing uncontrollably. Gabe heard her from the bedroom and quickly came out to check on her. Chloe hugged him and continued to let it all out. She appreciated that he wanted to try and console her, and she held onto him for dear life.

After a long, hard cry, she finally got up and headed for the bathroom. She blew her nose and washed her face and tried to splash some life into herself. Her eyes were swollen from crying, and her nose was bright red. She looked absolutely horrible. Her throbbing head only made matters worse. When she emerged from the bathroom, she was in a zombie-like state. Gabe wasted no time reminding her that it was noon, and he'd certainly enjoy a lunch time snack.

She picked up his special Mickey & Pluto bowl, a present from her last trip to Disney World and peeled a hard-boiled egg. She broke up the egg in the bowl, added a little spring water and swished it around. She placed it on his bone-shaped placemat, and he practically inhaled it. When he was done, he gently licked the bowl to make sure he had gotten every last crumb.

Chloe was always amazed at how tenderly he licked his bowl, how he showed such affection for his food. Despite her personal misery, Gabe was able to bring a smile to her face once again.

She mindlessly picked up his bowl once he was finished and washed it out in the sink. She thought to herself that she should call her parents and tell them what had happened. Though she didn't want to worry them or be a disappointment. She couldn't handle the pressure right now. Instead, she picked up the phone and dialed Grace's number. There was no pressure there.

Chloe wasn't surprised that Grace wasn't home, and she left a simple message. She didn't want to alarm her twice in one week. She had enough worries of her own with two kids and a husband.

Chloe found herself wandering around her apartment trying to figure out what to do with herself. She needed something to boost her spirits and decided to go to her bookcase where she kept several books of inspirational readings. When she scanned through the shelves, nothing really caught her interest, though. Then she came to a file that was propped up at the end of the bottom shelf. She grabbed it and tucked it under her arm She knew it was just what she needed. Her own inspiration.

She got comfy on the deck with Gabe on the lounge and began to go through the file that held copies of the sermons she had written when she served as Guest Pastor at her church the previous summer.

The reading soothed her nerves and reminded her to have faith and trust that all would work out for the best. Worry would only bring stress and negative energy. As she settled down and regained her confidence and composure, she became more and more convinced that she had been fired because she was getting closer to the truth. The truth that either Shannon, Theresa or both of them didn't want exposed.

Chloe felt like the answer was already very close to her. She just didn't know where to find it. With the realization that continuing to investigate Molly's death could put her own life at risk, she decided she had no choice but to push forward, dangerous or not. For some reason, she believed she was the one who was supposed to uncover the truth.

The answers were nearby, but she just couldn't seem to put her finger on them. What should she do next, she thought to herself. Look online for a new job, she decided, even though she still couldn't believe that she had been relieved of her duties at Dolphin Connection. Looking at opportunities just might boost her spirits, she reasoned, as she got up and made her way to her computer with Gabe on her heels.

She grabbed another glass of iced tea on the way, plopped into her desk chair and turned on her computer. She immediately googled marine mammal facilities in Florida and was impressed by the list reported. At this point, she had decided she would like to stay in Florida. She loved the area, and it had become her home. The new love interest in her life didn't hurt things either.

Chloe took her time looking through each of the websites for the facilities located in Florida. She was familiar with most of them. There were a couple of interesting options in The Keys, but she wasn't sure she really wanted to make The Keys a long-term home. It was a place she loved to visit, but not an area she'd want to settle down in for good.

She had saved the biggest, Ocean World, for last. Chloe looked throughout the facility's grant website and noticed that there was an opening available in the Research Department. Evidently, there was a special position that had been created to help the facility track their breeding practices among marine mammals. Ocean World was such a large operation that the sheer number of marine mammals in their care was phenomenal.

Chloe could see why they needed someone whose job it was to solely oversee the healthy, appropriate breeding practices of their animals.

This realization stopped her in her tracks. It was vital to the health of all animals that they only breed with other animals outside of their direct family lines. It was becoming harder and harder for smaller facilities like Dolphin Connection to have enough diversity among their population to continue with healthy breeding practices.

Chloe knew that Molly was actually looking into a voluntary "swap" program with other facilities so that each facility would be able to introduce some new blood lines among their own dolphins. In order to participate in this type of program, Chloe could only imagine that Molly would have needed to assemble a very clear catalogue of each of Dolphin Connection's dolphins and their blood lines, something like a family tree for humans.

The more she thought about it, the more she realized that Molly might have uncovered something troubling when she researched the individual backgrounds of the dolphins at Dolphin Connection. Could something, one small piece of information, be big enough to get her killed, Chloe wondered. Maybe, Chloe thought to herself, especially if that information could potentially lead to the demise of Dolphin Connection.

Without hesitation, she picked up the phone and got through to Luke Hayes, Molly's ex-boyfriend. He was at work in the Research Office so Chloe knew he couldn't speak freely. Luke had seemed suspicious to Chloe at first, but now she realized he was probably just scared. She hoped he could give her more insight into Molly's thought process while she was at Dolphin Connection.

"Luke, this is Chloe Martin. I know you can't talk openly since you are at work, but just answer me this one question."

"It's okay, Chloe, I'm alone right now. What do you want to know?"

"Why did you and Molly break up?"

"She became very secretive," he said. "I thought she might be seeing someone else because she wouldn't tell me what was bothering her. She finally started to tell me what was on her mind and made some devastating accusations about a prospective breeding plan at Dolphin Connection. I stopped her mid-conversation and told her that I was not interested in hearing anything further. My whole life I have dreamed of working with dolphins, and it was finally happening. I wasn't going to lose it all over some girl I just started dating."

"That's fine, Luke, but maybe you could have helped Molly and still kept your job."

Chloe hung up before he could respond. What a selfish coward, she thought to herself. She felt even worse for Molly knowing that she had reached out for help only to be turned away by someone she thought had feelings for her. It sounded as if she felt an urgency to resolve the breeding matter because it had not yet happened. That part was good news.

Chloe was more motivated than ever to figure out the whole mess.

Molly deserved that much. Chloe felt Molly would do the same if the situation was reversed. She had shown herself as a person of character by standing up for the dolphins and trying to do what was right. Chloe had too much faith in God's plan for her life to quit now. She continued to believe she had been the one to discover Molly's body for a reason. She had to press forward.

She then punched Brian's number into her iPhone and waited impatiently as it rang. They had plans for that evening, but it was only mid-afternoon. He wasn't supposed to come over to pick her up until 7 PM. Where could he be, she thought to herself? She knew this wasn't an emergency, but her patience with the whole situation had run out. She wanted to know who had killed Molly, and she wanted her life back. Being away from the dolphins was tearing her apart.

Knowing time always passed more quickly when she was busy, she decided to organize herself so that she would be ready to jump when Brian returned her call. Gabe was taken for a walk and fed and the kitchen was cleaned up. She even put on an evening outfit so she would be ready for her dinner with Brian and Eliza that night.

Having run out of things to do at home while she was waiting to hear from Brian, Chloe decided to head over to the bagel store for a very late lunch. She knew she still had a little time left before Ann and Greg closed for the day, and she knew they would be happy to fix her something and sit down for a chat.

"How's our girl doing?" called Greg from behind the counter as Chloe entered the bagel store.

"I've been better," she replied as she sat down at a nearby table.

"Aren't you supposed to be at work? Would something to eat help lift your spirits?" He asked as he finished an order for a young man waiting at the counter.

"I am supposed to be at work, but I'll tell you about that when we talk. Your food always helps cheer me up, so I won't turn it down. I'll take my afternoon usual, thanks."

Hearing Chloe's voice, Ann came out from the back of the store. She greeted her with open arms. The hug felt good, and Chloe held on a moment longer than usual.

"Sit down and tell me what's going on," Ann said as she motioned towards an empty chair. "How come your out of work so early?"

"When I arrived at work this morning, I was fired."

"You were what?!" Ann asked in disbelief.

"I was fired. I still can't believe it myself. Shannon and Theresa said that my services were no longer needed at Dolphin Connection, and they offered no explanation as to why they suddenly felt that way. Then they had me clear my belongings out of my desk and escorted me off the property."

Ann leapt out of her chair and embraced Chloe again. "How are you doing? Does Brian know?"

"I am hanging in there, just barely. Brian came over immediately this morning after it happened, and he assured me that everything would be okay. He thinks I must have made someone uncomfortable asking around about Molly's work and any connection it might have to her murder. When he left my apartment, he was on his way over to Dolphin Connection to question Shannon and Theresa again. That was a few hours ago, and now I need to speak to him urgently. I left him a few messages but haven't heard back yet."

"What's going on? Why do you need to speak to him so urgently?"

"When I was looking online for possible job opportunities this afternoon, I began thinking about the case again, and I just might have figured out what got Molly into trouble with her killer. It appears that she discovered some unsettling information about an upcoming breeding match at Dolphin Connection and wanted to halt the pairing before it happened."

"Well, Brian is a detective, after all, Chloe. Maybe it's best to leave these matters to him. If whatever Molly found out was sufficient to make someone angry or scared enough to murder her, that means your life could be in danger, too, if you keep digging around. It appears as if your interest in the case alone has already cost you your job."

"I know, Ann, and I am being careful. But, I can't just back off totally. A good person's life was taken, and that isn't right. I am confident that I'm supposed to help Brian figure out this mess. After all, I was the one who found Molly's body. In the end, I do believe I will have my job back as well. Right now, though, I wish I would hear back from him. I don't like sitting on information that could possibly help him solve this case."

"Maybe he got caught up in another case that has him cut off from outside communication. Molly's case isn't life threatening to anyone. Unfortunately, she is already dead. It's very possible that he simply planned to go over your lead with you this evening."

"That's true," Chloe agreed. "We do have dinner plans for this evening. It looks like I'll have to talk to him about everything then. I'm sure he just got caught up with something else and isn't intentionally avoiding my calls."

"Now, Chloe. Let's not jump the gun here. From everything you have said, Brian is a sweet, kind, trustworthy man. He sounds quite old-fashioned actually, much like Greg. That type of man is very hard to find nowadays and is worth holding onto and trusting for sure. The best thing you can do right now is to keep your chin up, have something to eat and look forward to seeing him tonight. In the meantime, let the man do his job."

Chloe smiled sheepishly at Ann, knowing she was right, but it was hard not to be insecure at this early stage of a relationship. She was relieved to see Greg heading in her direction with food. It provided a great opportunity to change the topic of conversation.

"The afternoon usual, on us," sang Greg cheerily as he placed Chloe's Everything Bagel sandwich, chips and drink in front of her.

"Thanks," she said. "But I can pay for my lunch. I've only been out of work for less than a day. I'm not that poor yet."

"Out of work, don't be silly. What is she talking about, Ann?"

As Ann concisely replayed Chloe's day, Greg was as shocked as they were to hear the news. He hugged Chloe tightly and put his hand under her chin so that he could look her into the eyes.

"Listen, Chloe, this is our treat because we are happy to see you twice in one day, not because you are temporarily out of work. Ann and I know that this nonsense will be straightened out soon, and you will be back on the docks with those dolphins where you belong before you know it."

"Thanks, Greg. You always know how to lift a girl's spirit."

Chapter 23

Chloe got back in her car feeling uplifted from her visit with Ann and Greg. She knew they were right about everything. Brian was an incredible man, and she couldn't wait to see him that night for dinner. She also knew she would be back home with her beloved dolphins soon.

Her heart ached at the thought of the dolphins, though. She knew they didn't understand her absence and worried that it might cause some of them — like Cali, Alexa, Sophie and Emma — undue stress. She needed to get back to her normal routine with them, and she needed to do it fast, for their sake, as well as her own. There was only one way that was going to happen and that would be by solving Molly's murder.

She pulled out her phone and dialed Bailey. She answered on the first ring.

"Hey, Bailey, it's me, Chloe."

"Chloe, how are you? I've been worried sick about you."

"I'm hanging in there. How are my dolphins?"

"They are hanging in there, too, but they seem to sense that things are not right. You know how perceptive they can be," Bailey said.

"That's the truth. They are smarter than us humans, that's for sure. Do you think they miss me?"

"You know they miss you. That's a given. Theresa has been covering for your sessions since she let you go, and she just doesn't seem to be on with them. The dolphins almost seem uneasy around her."

"That's odd," Chloe replied. "Theresa has always had a very strong relationship with the dolphin family at Dolphin Connection. Something just isn't right."

"You're right about that. Just this afternoon, Theresa received a call and stormed out of here. She never leaves haphazardly like that. We all know, until the recent changes, she follows the same routine each day. She leaves the facility at 5 PM and goes home for dinner. At 6 PM, she faxes over the next day's schedule to the last trainer on duty to hang up in the office before closing rituals. Then, she's off for a jog."

"The same thing, every day," Chloe responded.

"That's right. A ritual that we all know well, by the way," Bailey added.

"A ritual that is always followed, except on the night of Molly's death," Chloe revealed.

"What are you talking about?"

"On the evening of Molly's death, I was the last trainer on duty, and I lingered on the docks with the girls for even longer than usual. By the time I did my evening rounds and discovered Molly's body on the way, it was just before 7 PM when I ran into the Trainer's Office to dial 9-1-1. I remember because I was staring at the clock the whole time I was on the phone with the Emergency Operator. Theresa's fax was just coming in when I ran inside to use the phone. I remember listening to the machine humming along. I didn't remember to hang up the schedule during all of the excitement, so I never gave the timing of the fax another thought, but now it troubles me. Why did Theresa send the fax an hour late that evening? She always sticks to her schedule."

"That's true, but something could have come up that evening. You never know. Things happen sometimes," Bailey reminded her friend.

"Also true. But why did Theresa direct Brian to conduct his interviews of the staff as succinctly as possible? While she claims to be in support of the investigation, her actions are speaking far louder than her words! Maybe she was worried someone like Molly's boyfriend Luke might disclose information that would incriminate top management."

"You can't mean Theresa, Chloe. Dolphin Connection is her life. She loves the dolphins and all of the people who take care of them. She would never do anything to hurt the welfare of the facility," Bailey said.

"Bailey, how can you say that when she just fired me? She knows the dolphins mean the world to me, and she has forbidden me from setting foot on the grounds. She has torn my heart out without any reason. Because I found Molly's body, I feel a responsibility to help solve the murder. Theresa didn't have to fire me because I was trying to do the right thing."

"I know, I know," Bailey said, sounding as frustrated as Chloe was, "and I'm sorry if I hurt your feelings. Maybe you should just leave the police work up to the police, though, and focus on getting your job back. Detective White seems like he has his act together. This case will be solved by the proper authorities."

"You're right, Bailey, but it's hard for me to step back and let it go when I feel like I can really help. Brian and his colleagues have so much on their plates with all of the budget cutbacks, it's hard for them to focus on just one case. Brian's boss, the Chief of Police, actually had to pull his partner off the case to work on something else. That sort of makes me his unofficial partner."

"Let them do their jobs, Chloe, and please take care of yourself. You are not trained to investigate crimes. You are trained to train dolphins!"

"I will, I will. Now I've got to run because hopefully I still have a meeting with Brian and Eliza tonight to go over the Research Seminar. Eliza planned to point out to us any new information Molly had uncovered since she was in charge of the research material, though my revealing conversation with Luke this afternoon may already have solved the case."

"Sounds like this whole mess could come to a close soon. Have a wonderful night with Detective White," Bailey said. "And be careful!"

"I will. Take care of my dolphins for me."

"I will."

Chloe knew Bailey was right and tried to convince herself of this as she drove home to take care of Gabe before she went out for the evening. Something continued to nag at her, though, and just as she thought she could let it go, she made a U-turn and headed in the direction of Theresa's house.

Making a U-turn at rush hour with so many elderly drivers around was always dangerous, and Chloe almost didn't make it through the turn safely.

She hadn't heard from Brian and knew she was overstepping her bounds by going over to Theresa's house, but something pulled her in that direction anyhow. It was like the strong force of a magnet, and Chloe couldn't break the attraction. She just wanted to talk to Theresa about the seminar and the information Luke had mentioned earlier and then she would head home. She certainly wasn't going to accuse anyone of murder. She would leave the real police work to the Police. She simply wanted to understand why Theresa had turned on her.

Chloe had been to Theresa's house many times over the years and so had no problem finding it. It was tucked behind several, gorgeous banyan trees and set back on the property to afford a beautiful view of the Gulf of Mexico. The home always took Chloe's breath away with its magnificence.

She pulled up in the driveway and parked over to one side. There was another car in the driveway she thought she recognized, but couldn't place its owner at the moment. She thought to herself that maybe Theresa had company staying with her and maybe that was why she had rushed home from Dolphin Connection early that evening and broken her routine the night of Molly's murder. House guests always throw off your schedule.

Bailey was right, Chloe thought to herself. Things do happen. Maybe something very innocent happened the night of Molly's murder that kept Theresa from faxing the following day's schedule to the trainer's office on time.

Chloe shook her head as she realized that she was way out of line coming over to Theresa's house to question her about the research material she had uncovered and her conversation with Luke. She would bring everything to dinner that night and explain it to Brian and Eliza so that Brian, in his capacity as Detective, could move forward with the case properly. Brian might not know much about the breeding practices of dolphins, but he was a smart guy and he would catch on quickly. The intelligent thing to do was to head to her favorite bakery to pick up dessert for that evening and get home to Gabe as she had been doing before making this rash decision.

Just as she decided her new plan of action and began to set the research folder back down on her passenger seat, she felt a cold, metal object pressed against her neck. Chloe had never touched a gun before, but she was pretty sure that the object being pressed against her neck was indeed a gun.

"Pick up that folder and turn around slowly," said a cold, hard voice behind her. "Don't do anything stupid, or you'll regret it."

Chloe didn't recognize the voice at first because it was so angry, but as she slowly turned around holding the research materials as directed, she was not surprised to see Shannon.

"You just couldn't leave it alone, could you, Chloe? You had to keep digging until you ruined it for everyone."

"My only desire was to find the truth, to figure out what happened to Molly. She was a nice person, and she hadn't done anything wrong. She didn't deserve to die because she was doing her job."

"She overstepped her bounds, as you have today. She dug into information that was not her business. Just like you have. Why were you bringing the seminar notes over to Theresa's house? She fired you and told you to stay away from Dolphin Connection. It is unbelievable that she didn't have you return everything this morning," Shannon said.

"I hoped she might uncover the truth," spoke a nervous voice from beside the garage.

Both Chloe and Shannon turned, surprised to see that Theresa was standing next to the garage, quietly witnessing the whole scene.

Theresa continued, "I'm sorry for everything, Chloe. I never wanted to fire you. Shannon pressured me in a way that only a sister can. She threatened to call our father and have him sell the whole business. Shannon swore that you were somehow involved in Molly's murder being that you were the one that found her body and all. The facility and the dolphins are my life. I couldn't risk losing them. I just hoped the truth would come out about Molly's killer.

Though I had my suspicions, I never thought you could do this Shannon. I didn't think you had it in you. What was Molly researching that made you feel it was necessary to take her life?"

Chloe was nervous, being that she had a gun pointed at her, but she spoke up anyhow. She didn't have much to lose at that point. "From what I can determine, Molly found out that Shannon had planned an unethical breeding match. When she began to research the blood lines of our dolphin family, it became clear to her that the intended pairing could present serious health issues for their offspring. Molly wanted to make sure that the unhealthy match never occurred and that only safe breeding practices were followed at Dolphin Connection."

"Is this true?" Theresa asked her sister.

"That know-it-all Molly called me and asked me to come over to the facility that evening," Shannon said.

"That is why you asked me to pick up your kids from their swim practice that night?" Theresa said out loud as she started to sort things out.

"Yes. I knew Molly had uncovered something from the tone of her voice, and I wanted to shut her up immediately," Shannon fumed.

"And that's why you were late faxing over the trainer's schedule, Theresa. You had to pick up Shannon's kids. Your routine was broken," Chloe said, all the pieces of the puzzle beginning to fit into place.

"Chloe, I hope you didn't think I killed Molly," Theresa said with a tinge of bewilderment in her voice.

Chloe responded, "Everything seemed to point in your direction. Everyone knows that Shannon has a very minimal role in the day-to-day affairs of Dolphin Connection. Why was she even running the Research Department?"

"It was the one area I was most interested in and could oversee from home without having to be at the facility in person," Shannon offered.

"You had no idea about this intended breeding match, Theresa?" Chloe carefully asked, looking for answers, all the while trying not to get herself killed.

"Chloe, you must believe that I had no idea what was going on with the breeding practices. Shannon always focused on the research and medical side of the dolphins and monitored their mating interactions. I would never let anything go on that would jeopardize the health of our family members."

It was awfully naïve for Theresa to leave a matter as important as breeding practices solely to Shannon, Chloe thought to herself. She shook her head in disbelief and was quickly reminded of the gun being held to it.

"Stop moving your head," Shannon shouted at Chloe. "Theresa didn't know what I planned to do, and it would have been easy to hide the risks of the potential match from her. The dolphins involved were transferred to Dolphin Connection from another facility when that facility closed. Theresa would not have necessarily known that the dolphins I planned to mate were actually close relatives."

Chloe stared at her mentor in shock.

"Hard to believe, though believable, since you are so busy with the daily operations of Dolphin Connection. You should have been more careful, Theresa," Chloe offered disappointingly.

"I thought I could trust my sister, of all people," Theresa said.

"That's true," Chloe quickly affirmed. "One should always be able to trust her sister."

"You shouldn't have come here," Shannon barked angrily at Chloe. "You shouldn't have gotten involved in our family business."

"I'm sorry for all of this, Chloe," cried Theresa. "I really wish you hadn't come here, too."

"Well then that makes me number three," spoke a loud male voice emerging from around the deep shadows of the banyan tree. "I certainly wish you hadn't come here, Chloe. You should have waited for my call. Now, we are going to miss our dinner plans," Brian said gently to let her know he wasn't too mad at her and everything would be okay.

Chloe couldn't believe her eyes and neither could Shannon and Theresa. Brian must have crept quietly onto the property while the women were talking back and forth. Leave it to the jabber jaws of women to save her life, Chloe thought to herself.

"Put the gun down carefully and place your hands over your head," he ordered Shannon.

His voice was authoritative and firm, and Chloe wasn't surprised that Shannon immediately responded. She appeared to be almost relieved at that moment that it was all over.

Brian moved in effortlessly, handcuffed her and retrieved the gun from the ground. Chloe was sure that ballistics would prove that Shannon had indeed used this very weapon to end Molly's life. Those results would come in due time. For now, Chloe was simply relieved to no longer have that gun pointing at her own head.

"Both of you inside the house," Brian called to Chloe and Theresa as he walked Shannon across the long lawn and over to his squad car, which he had parked in front of the next-door neighbor's house. "Wait there, while I call for back up. And try not to get yourself in any more trouble, Chloe," he added as an afterthought.

As Chloe and Theresa walked inside together, Theresa apologized profusely for her actions. She revealed to Chloe that she had recorded Shannon's confession on her cell phone and hoped that it would help bring about justice for Molly. Theresa was distraught that her own sister had taken a life and deeply saddened that she may have been able to prevent it. Chloe reassured her that everything would be okay, though she wasn't quite sure how.

Chloe and Theresa sat together on the beautiful balcony off Theresa's first floor living space and sipped lemonade. They sat quietly and watched a pod of wild dolphins fish as the sun set in the distance. The fluid movements of the dolphins and their incredible beauty out in the open waters was therapeutic. They sat silently and drank in the positive energy that flowed from what they considered their human counterparts that lived in the water.

"Chloe, may I talk to you privately, please?"

Chloe turned around to see Brian motioning for her to come to him.

Theresa spoke up and offered that they could step inside the house for privacy.

Brian thanked Theresa and asked that she wait to be questioned herself.

Chloe was nervous as she knew the conversation between she and Brian would be a gut-wrenching one.

"What were you thinking coming out here alone?" He questioned as she shrank backwards. "You put yourself in grave danger, and you put me in a tough spot."

"I'm sorry," she replied, not really knowing what else to say. "I'm sorry for everything. I should have waited for you to return my call, to explain the information I uncovered so that all of this could have been handled safely and properly."

"If I hadn't been tied up with training all afternoon, I would have gotten back to you sooner. I happened to be on my way back to the station from the shooting range when I received your message. I stopped at the bagel shop to see if you were still there and fortunately caught Ann and Greg as they were closing the store. They had a funny feeling you had headed over to Theresa's house even though Ann had warned you to let it go and let me handle it. While we were talking, a call came in from Grace. She, too, was looking for you because she had a terrible feeling that you were in imminent danger. When you didn't answer your cell phone, she called Greg since it was the only other person's number she had on record. And by the way, you might want to give her my number."

"I heard the phone ring with my *Let It Go* tone, set specifically for Grace, while Shannon had the gun to my head. The tune made the situation sort of ironic," Chloe offered, sounding a lot more humorous than she felt. "The moment I heard the song, I certainly wished I had let it all go and driven straight home as planned to wait for you."

"Next time, and let's hope there isn't a next time…let it go and let me handle it! It's amazing though, that Grace knew pretty much the exact time you were in trouble," Brian said and shook his head in disbelief.

"I'm not surprised," Chloe replied. "She's not only my best friend, she's my twin sister. We've always known how each other was feeling during the happy and not so happy times. I'm sure Grace could feel my terror when that cold gun was first held to my neck."

"Thankfully, she did, because it pushed me to get here immediately."

"How did you find the house?" Chloe asked.

"I called Bailey, and she happened to be in the trainer's office. She gave me Theresa's address and confirmed that you might be on your way over here."

"Thank you for saving my life, Brian. In more ways than you know."

"And thank you for saving mine, too," he said and smiled in the sweet, sensitive way that touched Chloe's heart each and every time he did so.

"You are everything I've always wanted, Chloe, and I'm so happy we have found each other."

"I feel the same way," she said, relieved this was all over. "Funny how the scariest thing that has ever happened to me has become the greatest thing. Please forgive me if I haven't let you know how special you are. Your past is your past, and you don't need me to make you feel any worse about it. You have been nothing but supportive and acceptive of me. Seems like I was the one who forgot about trust today. Can you forgive me?"

"Only if you promise never to scare me like this again. Seeing you with a gun being held to your head made my stomach churn. It's hard to do your job when the woman you love is involved in the case. In the future, please leave the detective work to me!"

"I guess that means I can't be your unofficial partner any longer?"

"What does that mean?"

"Oh nothing," Chloe giggled, making no promises to retire. She could only imagine what interesting cases he might need assistance with in the future.

"Chloe," Brian retorted, "I'm counting on you to behave yourself. You take care of the dolphins, and I'll take care of the detective work."

"That's fair," she agreed. "Assuming that I'll once again have a job working with the dolphins."

“It will all work out, Chloe, I promise. As soon as this all gets sorted out, I’m sure you’ll be back where I found you that first night…down on the docks with your soul mates.”

“That is where I see myself, too,” she responded.

“That is what I love about you, Chloe. You are passionate in all you do and toward everyone you love. Always, stay that way.”

“That will always be me.” She smiled at him and then hugged the man whom she had come to love so dearly in such a short time. He understood her in a way that was truly a blessing. She would go to sleep that night knowing how much he cared for her, and he knowing that she thought the world of him.

He kissed her gently and looked her straight in the eyes. The look they shared confirmed their future together.

“Now let’s get you home safely, dolphin girl.”

After she briefly said goodnight to Theresa, Brian walked Chloe down to her car. She handed the folder she had in her car to him as it would now be evidence along with the crucial information that Luke had mentioned, and the confession that Theresa had recorded. Brian instructed one of the junior officers to make sure she got home safely.

Epilogue

The wedding had been perfect in every way. Not because every detail had gone as planned, but because Chloe had married the perfect man.

Though there had been bumps in the road along the way, the trust that had built between them as their relationship unfolded had paved the way to real happiness.

Reciting their vows on the dock where they had first met made the event both unique and special, as well as a little rocky due to the fact that the dock was a floating one.

They were surrounded by loved ones from near and far. Their families had flown in for the big event and relished spending so much time getting to know one another.

Of course, Grace had been Chloe's Maid of Honor, and Brian's oldest brother had been his Best Man. Having her twin at her side on her Wedding Day meant that everything went smoothly without Chloe having to utter a word. Grace had always known what Chloe needed and wanted.

When Chloe and Brian kissed following their vows, the girls in the lagoon started doing dives and flips as if they had been given a signal to do so. The calves Alexa and Sophie had grown considerably by then and joined in for the exuberant celebration. The squeaks and clicks from their blowholes sent the crowd into an uproar.

Everyone clapped and cheered, waving their wedding bandanas which had been beautifully painted by all of the dolphins with the help of their trainers. The motion of the waving bandanas along with the excited noise from the guests sent the dolphins racing, diving and flipping around their lagoon. Things got so excited and the floating dock so wobbly, Chloe worried that she, Brian and the Minister might end up in the water with the dolphins. Now that would have been a scene!

The reception afterwards was held on the balcony at Theresa's house.

Theresa had continued on under her father's guidance as the President of Dolphin Connection. She had asked Chloe to be her Vice President of Operations, and Chloe had gladly accepted. Her only requirement was that her day-to-day interactions with the dolphins remain the same.

Chloe and Theresa had become closer in the months following that fateful night and when Theresa offered her house for the reception, Chloe gladly accepted. It was Theresa's way of making amends for all that had happened.

Chloe hadn't held Theresa responsible for Shannon's actions, because she understood the bond of sisterly love. Chloe was grateful that her sister always had her best interest in mind. Theresa had not been so fortunate.

The whole staff of Dolphin Connection had attended the wedding which made it a real family celebration. Bailey looked stunning and was thrilled to not only be the new Head Trainer, but also the girlfriend of Ken Sherman, the junior officer who had escorted Chloe home from Theresa's house that fateful night.

Nobody commented on the absence of Luke Hayes from the Research Department. He had quietly been let go from his position following the show down with Shannon. Both Theresa and Chloe agreed that he had placed his own desires ahead of the welfare of the dolphins and Molly, and that was not the type of person they wanted on their staff.

The only reminder of Shannon was a picture Theresa still kept hanging in the dining room. A photographer had captured them together interacting with several of the dolphins at the opening day of the facility. A newspaper clipping of the event had been framed with the picture. Chloe understood that Theresa kept the picture on the wall because it was a reminder of the dream she and her sister had once shared — a bond of sisterly love that could not be broken.

Shannon had yet to go to trial for Molly's murder, but things did not look good for her. Much evidence had been amassed.

Rumors had emerged that Shannon's husband had left she and her three children in financial ruin when his business failed weeks prior to Molly's murder. Her worries over her family situation clearly impacted her decisions with the dolphins. She had let her husband's actions drive her own.

Shannon later admitted that she had made a mistake when she planned to allow inbreeding to occur among the dolphins at Dolphin Connection.

She had actually come clean about her intentions the night she and Molly met. She tried to explain to the young researcher that she felt pressure to create more offspring for their dolphin family, and faced difficulty because they had exhausted all other possible matches for mates. Molly pointed out that lending practices were occurring between facilities to broaden blood lines, and Dolphin Connection would eventually make it to the top of those waiting lists. Shannon had impatiently felt that it would take too long for a small facility like Dolphin Connection to be chosen for a dolphin swap.

Shannon was going to speak with Theresa about everything the day she was approached by Molly. She felt threatened by Molly's discovery and reacted in fear. She drove home after their discussion that evening, picked up the gun her husband left behind and returned to Dolphin Connection to find Molly. The fact that she had premeditated the event made the charges against her murder rather than manslaughter.

Out of everything comes something else entirely, though. Because of what had happened to Molly, Chloe and Brian had met. Chloe hoped that somewhere Molly was smiling down knowing that her death had brought forth something beautiful and good.

Her family was relieved to know what had actually happened and hoped that justice would prevail at Shannon's trial. They were touched that Chloe and Theresa commissioned a beautiful sculpture of a dolphin riding on the wings of an angel to be made and dedicated to Molly. It stood in front of the Research Department where Molly spent most of her time.

Molly had died a hero trying to protect the lives of the beautiful grey faces that graced the waters of Dolphin Connection each day. She would not be forgotten, and her work would be diligently remembered.

Finishing up an afternoon training session with her favorite girls, Chloe was in the water and surrounded by their beautiful faces at that very moment. Cali had been allowing Chloe to have contact with the twins for some time now and both girls were very fast learners. She had spent most of the session buzzing and clicking and making her unique dolphin sounds all over Chloe's tummy, quite intent on communicating a message to Chloe, and Chloe smiled knowingly at her dolphin sister.

"I know, I know, Cali. I think you are right, but let's wait for the doctor to confirm our prediction this afternoon."

Chloe had been feeling a little different that week, and she was pretty sure she was pregnant. She had scheduled an appointment with her doctor that afternoon to find out if she was right.

Cali kept right on nudging Chloe's tummy and making noises in two very distinct areas.

"You think so, sweetie? I hadn't really thought about it until now, but twins do run in the family. Maybe there are two babies in there."

Wouldn't that be a blessing, Chloe thought to herself. She couldn't think of anything more special than the bond she and Grace shared. How wonderful it would be for her own children to have that. If it were true, Chloe would be so excited to call Grace with the news. But then again, knowing Grace, she already knew.

The big surprise would be for Gabe. He had just gotten used to having Brian living with them, and now, he'd be joined by two little babies.

And Brian…he'd be so excited to have not one, but two babies. He was in awe of the relationship that Chloe and Grace shared. He would be thrilled to watch his own children share the same bond.

"It all started here on these docks and now it continues!" Chloe shared with Cali. "Let me do as good a job as you have as a mother Cali, and we'll all be fine." Chloe looked deep inside the eyes of this amazing creature in front of her and saw only love and understanding. They each recognized the love they shared between them and knew it was something special.

"I've gotta go girls," she called to the dolphins as she somewhat gracefully pulled herself up onto the dock, starting to worry that a twin pregnancy might be more than her body could handle.

From behind, she felt a large splash and turned around to find a playful Emma drenching her with more and more water. Chloe smiled at the loving Aunt Emma acknowledging that she understood the message. “You’re right, Miss Emma, relax and enjoy the ride, and it will all turn out fine.”

Chloe knew in her heart at that moment that all was well, times two!

The destiny of her life had circled around to greet her once more.

Dolphin Fun Facts

- Dolphins belong to the Order Cetacea and the Family Delphinidae. The Orca, or killer whale, is the largest member of the family which is made up of over 30 different species.
- Many people around the world recognize the Atlantic Bottlenose Dolphin whose scientific name is Tursiops Truncatas. Bottlenose dolphins are found in many diverse types of waters across the world.
- Dolphins can be identified by their dorsal fin. Variations in the dorsal fin help us recognize an individual dolphin like the features of the face for a human. The tail flukes of a dolphin are also unique and can help a trainer identify a specific dolphin; similar to the handprints and footprints of people.
- The dorsal fin on a dolphin's back is used for stability. Their pectoral fins are for steering. Their tails provide great propulsion through the water and are enormously strong.
- Dolphins are marine mammals. They have belly buttons because they are connected by an umbilical cord in utero like humans. Dolphins breathe air through their blow hole located on top of their head, and they have whiskers around their rostrum when they are first born. A dolphin mother produces milk in order to nurse her calf.

- Dolphins can dive to great depths of up to 200 to 250 feet, though most tend to limit dives to shallow depths of roughly 10 feet hunting for fish along the shorelines. A US Navy dolphin named Tuffy made an incredible dive over 900 feet!
- Dolphins usually stay underwater for an average of 8 to 10 minutes.
- Dolphins can swim at burst speeds of up to 25 to 30 mph, although it is more common for them to swim along at 7 to 8 mph.
- Dolphins only rest one half of their brain at a time when they sleep.
- The average life span of an Atlantic Bottlenose Dolphin in the wild is roughly 25 years. Some in human care have lived up to 40 or 50 years.
- Dolphins receive all of their water intake from the fish they eat. If a dolphin stops eating for any reason, the dolphin will become dehydrated quickly which can be very dangerous.
- Atlantic Bottlenose Dolphins use their 88 to100 conical shaped teeth to grab their prey. Then they swallow their fish whole in order to squeeze the water out.
- Dolphins eat their fish head first. This keeps the fin and spines of the fish folded back in such a way that they won't hurt the dolphin's throat.
- Dolphins eat various types of fish including herring, grouper, mackerel and sardines. At dolphin facilities and aquariums, dolphins eat restaurant-quality fish that is thoroughly checked and cleaned before it reaches a dolphin's mouth.
- It is important that dolphins in human care have "dolphin time" when there are no trainers or visitors

around. This allows them to interact with each other without outside expectations.

- Dolphins live in social groups called pods. There are maternity pods which consist of mature females and calves, juvenile pods that are made up of males and females that are not sexually mature, and bachelor pods whose members are adult males. Some males become very close, similar to best friends for people. They are called pair-bonded. A pod can range from 2 to 30 members. It is an awe-inspiring sight to see dolphins in the wild hunting for fish in a pod and caring for their young.
- Research has shown that mature male and female dolphins do not live together as a family in the wild. Adult males seek out maternity pods to mate with adult females and then they quickly leave. Males practice intercourse on one another so that they will be efficient when they meet up with females and don't make themselves prey to sharks, etc. It is then solely the job of the mother to raise her calf with the help of the other females in the maternity pod.
- Dolphins normally give birth to one calf at a time. This way a pregnant female only develops a slight bulge in her belly area and stays streamlined in the water. Twin pregnancies are possible, though highly unlikely and result in challenging deliveries. Calves are born tail first (their tail is curled up) and when their head/blow hole emerges, the dolphin mother must nudge the calf to the surface quickly in order for it to take a breath.
- When a dolphin calf nurses, the calf will swim in the slipstream of the mother dolphin. The calf benefits by swimming very close in proximity to the mother with the center of his body aligned with her tail. The calf moves along more quickly by riding the wake of the

mother. From this location, the calf can insert its tongue, curled into a straw like shape, into the slit of the dolphin mother's mammary gland. Dolphin calves usually nurse for 1 to 3 years.

- Dolphins have a type of sonar called echolocation. This allows them to locate objects that are in their surroundings by sending out sound waves which bounce off the object and then return to the dolphin's melon (forehead) to relay information.
- Dolphins each have unique and interesting personalities. It's exciting when working with dolphins to get to know each one personally and discover their likes and dislikes.
- The signature whistle of a dolphin is like an individual name that affords dolphins the ability to recognize one another and be identified by humans.
- Dolphins have exceptional hearing even though they don't have external ears. Tiny pinholes located behind their eyes enable them to hear sounds over long distances.
- Dolphin vocalizations are extensive and can include whistles, clicks, chirps, pulsed sounds, squeaks and squeals. Dolphin training sessions can be quite a concert!
- Dolphins need both physical and intellectual stimulation on a daily basis. Training sessions allow dolphins to be challenged through exercise and problem-solving situations. If you visit a dolphin facility, you may see a dolphin recognize a shape or symbol that has been assigned to him or her. Through practice, the dolphin will identify and respond to his/her individual symbol.

- In general, Atlantic Bottlenose Dolphins are about 3 1/2 feet when they are born and weigh between 22 to 44 lbs. Mature adult males and females range in size and can grow up to 10 plus feet and weigh between 300 and 1,400 lbs.
- Though they may seem similar, most facilities use their own set of signals to work with their dolphins. That means a trainer who makes a move from one facility to another may have to learn new signals or use a different style of whistle to bridge. If you want to become a trainer, it is important that you work at a facility where you are comfortable with the overall policies and philosophical approach that pertain to the animals and the employees.
- Many trainers will conduct sessions with their dolphins from a platform or a floating dock that gets them very close to the dolphins, but not actually in the water with them. At other times, trainers will get right in the water with the dolphins to work on interactive behaviors like dorsal pulls that are sometimes used during a dolphin swim program or dolphin show. In-water time allows trainers to develop an even closer relationship with the dolphins in their own environment. It's important to be a very strong swimmer if you want to become a dolphin trainer, and it's also helpful to become scuba certified.
- In training sessions, positive behaviors are encouraged and acknowledged with a verbal and or physical interaction and a desired food source. This could be the whistle or the voice with dolphins, and, of course, fish. Further encouragement can include cheers and back rubs! Unwanted behavior is simply ignored.
- Dolphins have a complex systems of nerve endings which make their skin very sensitive to the touch. If

you are fortunate enough to enjoy a dolphin swim at an accredited facility, you will probably spend some time giving the dolphins you interact with pectoral rubs and back rubs. It can be a truly magical moment when you first touch a dolphin!

- If you want to become a dolphin trainer, start researching the facilities that exist in Florida and across the country. Most facilities offer volunteer and internship programs to people of various ages. Several facilities also offer specialized classes so that you can further your knowledge of marine mammals in general and receive more hands-on interaction. Many dolphin trainers have a background in either biology or psychology and sometimes both. If it is your dream to work with dolphins, go for it!
- Joining and training to be a part of a dolphin stranding team through a local aquarium or organization can be a wonderful way to help marine life. Living in an area where dolphins are prevalent will mean more opportunities on a local level. Sometimes though, dolphins and other marine mammals, like manatees, need help far from their usual waters because of strange weather patterns/storms, unhealthy water conditions, quickly changing tides or illness. The goal of rescue is always to rehabilitate and return an animal to his/her natural habitat. In cases in which an animal is not strong enough to return to the wild due to extensive injuries, health impairments or age, the corresponding government agency will select the appropriate marine life facility that can best meet the needs of the particular animal and give it a forever home.
- The National Oceanic and Atmospheric Administration (NOAA) recommends maintaining a minimum distance of 50 yards from any marine mammal in the wild.

Feeding any marine mammals in the wild is illegal and can be extremely dangerous to the health of the animals. The Marine Mammal Protection of 1972 was signed into law on October 21, 1972 by President Richard Nixon and went into effect on December 21, 1972. In summary, the law forbids the collection of marine mammals and makes illegal the import, export and sale of marine mammals, their parts, or products made from their parts, within the United States. The enforcement of the regulations stated within the MMPA is an important part of the law. See the website of NOAA Fisheries for a detailed and complete description of the MMPA.

Related Sources

https://www.dolphins.org
https://www.nationalgeographic.com
http://www.noaa.gov

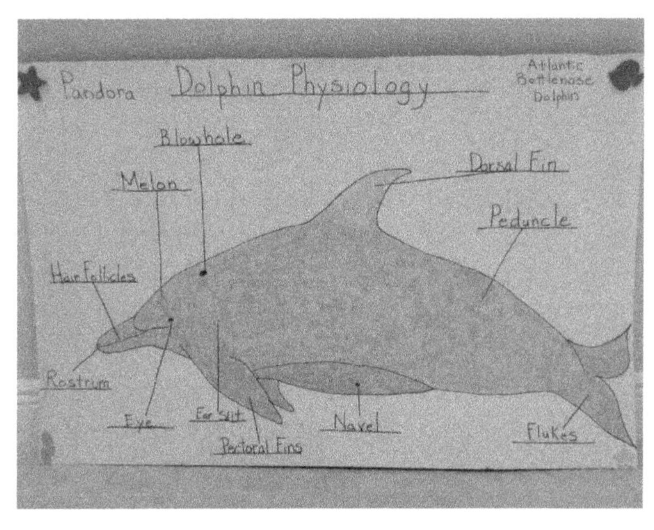

About the Author

Tracey V. Williams resides in Lakewood Ranch, Florida with her husband, twin daughters and poochon. She has her Masters in Teaching for Secondary Education and a Graduate Certification in American Art from Sotheby's Auction House. Over the years, Tracey has enjoyed teaching Social Studies to middle school students, sharing her love of dolphins with visitors at a marine mammal facility, leading school groups on tours of Colonial Williamsburg and having the opportunity to educate her own children. Tracey's passion for writing began in childhood and continues to grow each year.

For more information on the author and her books, please visit www.traceyvwilliams.com and join her on FaceBook: Tracey Williams.
Pinterest: www.pinterest.com/traceyvwilliams
Instagram: www.instagram.com/traceyvwilliams

Books by Tracey V. Williams

Dolphin Trainer Mysteries
Dolphin Girl
Dolphin Duo - coming soon!

Children's Picture Books
"GO BACK TO BED!"

Ninja the Penguin Series (Children's Chapter Books)
The Great Escape (Book 1) - coming soon!

"I write books that I would assign as a teacher and that I would recommend as a mom."

-*Tracey V. Williams*

CPSIA information can be obtained
at www.ICGtesting.com
Printed in the USA
LVHW032305171218
600835LV00002B/579/P